PIERCED Peony

DAHLIA DONOVAN

TANGLED TREE PUBLISHING

\-

\-

For information, contact the publisher, Tangled Tree Publishing.

www.tangledtreepublishing.com

Editing: Hot Tree Editing

Cover Designer: BookSmith Design

E-book ISBN: 978-1-922359-55-1

Paperback ISBN: 978-1-922359-57-5

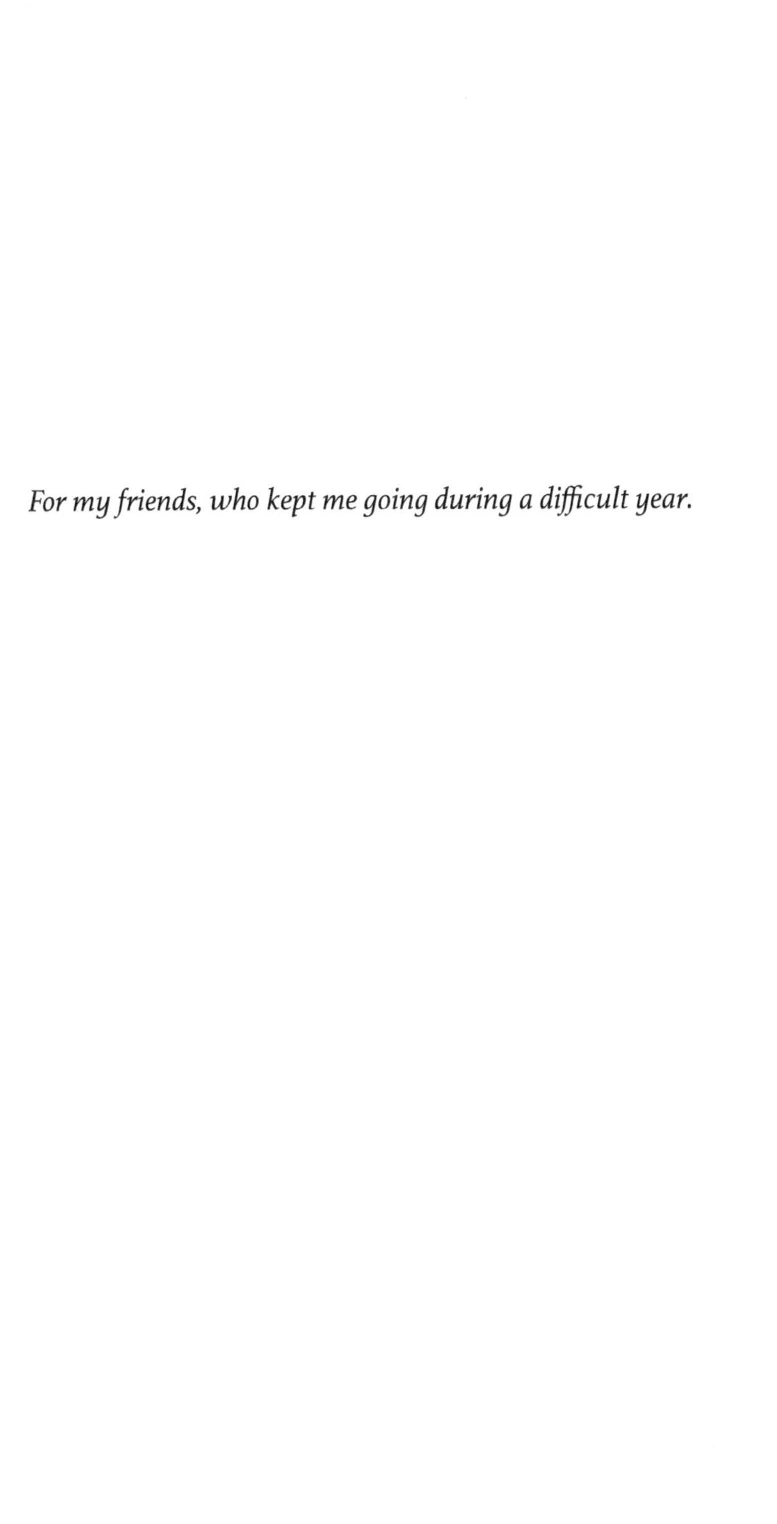

For my friends, who kept me going during a difficult year.

Chapter One

A CAT, A TURTLE, AND A STRANGER FACE OFF IN THE garden. The stranger blinks first. Right. The joke still needs some work.

"Do you always let your turtle and cat out in the garden together?"

"They're friends. They like to gossip." Motts set her trowel to one side and got to her feet. She dusted the grass and dirt off her knees. "They both need fresh air and sun in moderation. Are you lost?"

The man didn't seem lost despite having popped up beside the back fence around her garden. He looked like a police officer. Though not quite as broad-shouldered, he stood as tall as Teo Herceg, the detective inspector she'd met in April and had been dating for over a month.

"I'm hoping to speak with Pineapple Mottley." He sounded like a policeman. His suit, while nice, appeared rumpled from driving; his short grey hair, however, was gelled and styled perfectly. "I'm Detective Inspector Dempsey Byrne with the Metropolitan Police's cold case unit."

"Cold case?" Motts's heart stuttered in her chest. She rubbed her fingers together nervously. "Jenny. You're here about Jenny."

Jenny Cleverly had been her lone best friend through her early childhood. Motts had stumbled across Jenny's lifeless body on her way home from primary school while walking through a park, hidden behind a hedge. She still had nightmares about finding her.

The unsolved crime had haunted Motts. She'd developed an obsessive curiosity about cold cases as a result. And at least once a year, she searched online to see if anyone had been arrested for Jenny's murder.

"Ms Mottley?"

"Motts." She had a sudden sense of déjà vu; she'd had a similar conversation with Teo in April. He'd been investigating the murder of a Rhona Walters, who'd been buried in the garden behind her cottage. It had been an auspicious start to her life in Polperro. "*Cactus.*"

Her beloved Sphynx cat had leapt onto the fence and then over to the detective's shoulder. Detective Inspector Byrne didn't bat an eyelid. He simply reached up to pat Cactus on his head.

Well, he certainly approves of the random strange man intruding on our afternoon.

Intruding inspector intrudes introspectively.

Introspectively?

Not my best alliteration.

"I don't often see a flowerless garden." He glanced slowly around at her rows of fruits and herbs. "None at all?"

"My allergies try to drown me if I'm around them for too long." Motts kept flowers far away from her cottage. Real ones, in any case. She made and sold origami and quilled floral arrangements as part of her small business, Hollyhock Folded Blooms. "Why don't you come in for tea? Cold case curiosities can converse comfortably."

Don't frighten the fancy London detective with your peculiarities.

The judgmental voice in her head sounded suspiciously like her mum, who meant well but couldn't always relate to Motts's more unique traits.

She didn't understand her wayward autistic and asexual daughter. Motts had given up trying to fit into neurotypical moulds.

I am who I am.

Alliterations and all.

Oh, fun accidental alliterations are the best.

"I wouldn't want to impose."

"Wouldn't you?" Motts stared blankly at the man, unable to decide if he was being polite or not. "You drove from London. At least a five-hour drive on a good day. Tea isn't imposing. Sleeping in my garden and trampling the herbs would be."

Lifting Moss, her box turtle, up from where she'd been wandering around the garden, Motts headed toward the back door. She had no doubts Cactus would guide the detective inspector. Her cat had obviously claimed the man.

Why is my cat obsessed with brooding police types?

Is he trying to tell me something?

Do detectives smell like catnip?

Motts placed Moss into the terrarium, which took up most of the space in front of the large window facing the garden. It offered her turtle suffi-cient sunlight. "How do you take your tea?"

"In a mug."

Motts stared blankly at him. She barely managed

to decipher when her friends were teasing her, never mind a stone-faced detective. "I mostly use mugs. Teacups are too delicate."

"Just a dash of milk," he said kindly.

Motts grabbed the green beanie that River, her younger cousin, had bought for her a few weeks ago. It had become a fast favourite, her preferred colour and soft enough it didn't bother her fingers. She pulled the hat over her head to keep her shoulder-length brown hair out of her eyes. "You were joking."

Her cousin had recently moved to Polperro from Looe, where he'd lived with his parents and next door to their grandparents, into a flat with his boyfriend, Nish, one of Motts's best friends and the brother of her ex-girlfriend. They all hung out several times a week. She'd appreciated their support over the past few months.

The change from the hustle and bustle of London into a quiet cottage above the village had been a relief.

But still strange.

"I know. I don't seem the type." He took her confusion in stride, which she appreciated. "Does your cat usually wear a T-shirt in the summer?"

"And a cardigan in winter." Motts finished doling out snacks for both of her pets. She set Cactus's treat by the terrarium. The two loved to eat their afternoon snacks together. "He's delicate when it comes to sunlight and temperature."

He followed her into the kitchen, stepping back when she frowned at him. "You keep checking your watch. Am I holding you up?"

"I usually walk down to the village before tea." Motts kept to her routine religiously. It helped ease her anxiety.

"A walk through the village is a little public for what I'd like to ask you." Detective Inspector Byrne peered through the living room toward the window and out into the garden. "Doesn't the coastal path run along the side of your property? Why don't we hike for a bit?"

Motts's breath caught sharply in her throat. She hadn't dared stray too far down the path running alongside her fence. "I'm not sure if police gossip like villagers. A few months ago, I had a run-in with a murderer. They cornered me down by the lighthouse, and I almost tumbled off the cliff into the sea. I haven't managed to force myself out that way ever since."

"Fear's only going to amplify the longer you let it fester." He leaned against the side of her little kitchen table. "Three years ago, I chased a suspect on foot across a busy street. A car sent me flying. It took me well over twelve months to recover fully from all of my injuries. And even longer to escape the fear of being struck again. I flinched at car horns and screeching tires for the longest time."

"Face the fear?"

"Again and again through gritted teeth until you beat the bastard." Detective Inspector Byrne offered a gentle smile that reminded her of her uncle Tom in how much it put her at ease. "I'm an officer of the law. Why don't I walk you down the garden path?"

"You read a lot of fiction, don't you?" Motts gripped the kitchen counter, staring down at the box of tea she'd pulled out of the cupboard. "You sound like you swallowed an entire collection of literature."

He barked out a surprised laugh, shaking his head. "Your dad warned me to expect the unexpected with you."

"Did he?" Motts waved him off when he went to reply. "Right. If I stand here much longer, I'll throw off my routine. Let's walk. It's a mild enough summer day."

And if I don't move, I'll never get myself out of the cottage and down the path.

"You might want to exhale," he commented when they reached the garden gate.

Motts had held her breath while locking up the cottage and engaging the security system Teo had installed for her. She forced herself to breathe in deeply, enjoying the mild breeze coming off the sea. It smelled like heaven to her. "I did."

A few steps away from her garden gate, Motts considered the wisdom in going for a walk with a stranger. He hadn't even shown her any form of identification. She watched him out of the corner of her eye in silence for a few minutes.

"How do I know you're actually a detective?"

He reached into his pocket and retrieved his wallet, flipping it open to show his identification. "Maybe ask before you wander away from the safety of your cottage?"

Motts shoved her hands into her hoodie. She'd grabbed her favourite on the way out of the cottage; even in the summer, the breeze off the sea could get chilly. "Tell me about Jenny's case."

Anything to distract me from the irrational fear gnawing at my belly.

Is it irrational when I did almost plunge to my death?

"Our cold case unit was given twelve specific cases to focus on for the year. Hers was assigned to me. I've read up on the file. We've sent her clothing out to the lab. Forensics has come a long way since they were last tested." He paused to wait for her to catch up with his long strides. "I hope to re-interview all of the potential witnesses and those close to Ms Cleverly."

"My memory's spotty on the day itself. I remember flashes. Jenny hadn't been at school. I thought maybe her parents had kept her home. They sometimes did. We always walked through the park to get home. I remember seeing her coat. Bright blue. Under one of the bushes." Motts wrapped her arms around herself. "I was the only person in the park as far as I know."

"Did she have a boyfriend?"

"Boys were gross at that stage."

"Any trouble with her parents?"

Motts rubbed her arms, trying to focus on the question and not the lighthouse in the distance. "Maybe? We never talked about it. I don't always notice things other people might. We weren't at her house very often. Her father scared me."

The further down the path they went, the worse and yet also better Motts felt. She thought her heart might leap out of her chest when they reached the steps leading down to Spy House Point. It took all of her strength and courage to make her way down the stairs toward the safety railing.

A brisk summer breeze kicked up. Motts forced herself to peer down towards the waves crashing against the rocky shoreline. She glanced over at something being carried along by the sea.

What the... what is that?

"There's a body." Motts grabbed onto the railing when her knees buckled.

Detective Inspector Byrne rushed over to stand beside her and offered his arm for support. He stared down toward the rocky coastline. "What?"

"A body. There's a body in the sea."

Chapter Two

"I'M NEVER WALKING THE COASTAL PATH AGAIN. EVER. It's cursed." Motts huddled on the small bench at the top of the stairs, grumbling under her breath. She shivered despite the warm afternoon sun. "Oh yes, walking is brilliant for you. All the dead bodies are wonderful for my mental health."

"Ms Mottley? Motts?"

"Inspector Ash." She tried to muster a smile for him. "How's your Marnie?"

Detective Inspector Perry Ash was one of the few police officers based in their little village. Life in Polperro was so different from being in London. His wife, Marnie, ran the local bridal shop; she'd become good friends with Motts and frequently sold her paper bouquets to her customers.

"Hughie's going to help you home. It looks like you could use a warm cuppa, but don't let him make it. He'll burn your tongue off and put hairs on your chest." He waved toward the tall teddy bear of a constable, who'd been one of the first people to greet her when she arrived in the village. "The fancy London detective can answer my questions for now."

How does a cup of tea put hairs on your chest?

"Be nice. We can't all be born in Cornwall. I might've been, but neither of my grandparents were. They settled here from Jamaica." Hughie nudged the inspector with his elbow before offering his arm to Motts. "Don't you listen to the inspector. I'm a dab hand at making the perfect pot of tea."

"The wolves are going to descend."

"Wolves?"

"Vina, Nish, River, and probably even Marnie." Motts knew her friends and cousin had probably already heard about the excitement. News travelled faster than the wind in a little village. "Maybe you can protect me?"

"From Marnie Ash? I'd sooner take a header off the cliff. Terrifying woman." Hughie grinned at her. "Nothing wrong with your friends circling around you. We're a small village. We care about each other.

They're more like overexcited puppy dogs and not wolves."

Motts shrugged a shoulder and kept her gaze focused on the well-trodden dirt trail. "They'll hover—again."

"Well, you did stumble on another body."

"I didn't exactly walk into the first one." She didn't consider digging up a body in a garden stumbling. "I hope this doesn't become a trend."

They made it back to her cottage in no time at all. Hughie played sentry by the door while she got the kettle going. He staunchly refused tea but did sneak a few biscuits from the tin.

No amount of tea or lemon curd on toast could erase the vision of the body in the sea. Motts curled up on her sofa with Cactus, a blanket, and a second cup. Hughie left her alone to head into the village.

I wonder how long it'll be before the reinforcements he's going to summon arrive.

Cactus remained resolutely in her lap, refusing to budge. He hadn't even attempted to steal a sip of her tea or a bite of toast. She gently massaged his head and ears.

"We seem to have wandered into yet another mystery." Motts glanced down at Cactus when he meowed loudly. "Agreed. A second snack is in order.

We're going to need a distraction if your aunties and uncle descend on the cottage at the same time."

To her surprise, Hughie returned with only one person. He was carrying a tray. Marnie followed behind him; she immediately came over to offer Motts a hug, which she graciously turned onto Cactus when Motts waved her off. "Are you okay?"

"Fine." Motts peered curiously at the covered tray. "What'd you bring?"

"Cake," Hughie answered for Marnie. He lifted the lid off and offered one of the brightly coloured citrusy treats. "Think she made a bastardised version of the Maria Luisa cake."

"He's been watching *Bake Off* again," Marnie teased.

When his phone rang, Hughie set the tray down on the coffee table and stepped outside to answer. Marnie and Motts both stayed quiet, trying to listen in to whatever update he was getting.

Hughie rolled his eyes knowingly at them when he stepped into the cottage. He pocketed his phone. "We've called in Detective Inspector Herceg from the cold case unit in Plymouth."

"Cold case?" Motts ignored Cactus who'd leapt up into her arms. "How? I found the body a few hours ago in the sea."

"We've identified the body already. The victim disappeared three years ago. I shouldn't be telling you this without DI Ash's permission."

"How did a person who went missing three years ago wind up in the sea today?" Marnie's question echoed the one in Motts's mind. "It's highly unlikely to have been bashing about in the sea for so long only to suddenly appear now."

Motts agreed with her assessment. She'd seen enough of the body to think the person had been killed within the past twenty-four hours—not years ago. "Who were they?"

"Can't say." Hughie shook his head and cut Marnie off with a mock stern glare. "My lips are sealed. You can ask your husband. He's on his way."

Steeling herself to deal with loads of people, Motts went into the kitchen to start the kettle. She pulled down her mismatched mugs. Inspector Ash wouldn't be the only person to descend on her cottage.

Given the time of day, Griffin Brews, the coffee shop run by Nish, Vina, and their parents, wouldn't be too busy. The twins would come running to check on her, probably with food. Their mum, Leena, always wanted to feed everyone.

Must be a mum thing. Everyone's mum always seems

convinced none of us knows how to feed ourselves.

Of everyone in the village, Motts had known the Griffins the longest. She'd met them years ago when she'd come on holiday with her parents. Her mum and dad had originally come from Cornwall, and they'd spent many vacations all along the coast over the years.

Cadan Griffin had met his wife in India when he'd been a dashing Cornish-Indian cricket player, and she'd turned his head as a glamorous Bollywood star. They'd returned to his mum's hometown to open their bakery. Their twins, Pravina and Anish, had become instant friends with Motts when they'd met as children.

Never imagined years later we'd be ex-girlfriends turned into best friends living in the same village.

Faced with yet another murder mystery.

At least this one wasn't buried in my garden.

"I best get back to the shop." Marnie interrupted her thoughts. She was pocketing her phone while she got to her feet. "Take your time with the cakes. I've plenty of those trays. My mum-in-law keeps finding them for me. Why she thinks I need thirty of the blasted things, I'll never know."

"Marnie."

"You just settle in for a cosy afternoon." Marnie

inched towards the door.

"*Marnie*." Motts had to carefully set her tea down and dislodge Cactus before racing after her friend. She caught up to Marnie as she opened the door. "Well, hello, you three."

Vina dragged her into a hug, sending a poof of flour into the air. "We rushed from the café."

"I can tell." Motts pushed her away, then brushed off the dusting of white on her arms. "Maybe a change of clothes before you rush over to invade my space?"

"Rude. Ungrateful wretch." River eased between them, dragging Nish, his boyfriend of several months, behind him. "And here we all abandoned work at the drop of a hat for you."

"You love us despite our mess." Vina had dusted off the flour and gathered her long black hair into a loose bun. Motts turned as she went to follow River and Nish toward the kitchen. "My brother and your cousin have reached the disgusting sweet nothing stage of their relationship. You should've heard them on the drive up to the cottage."

"Says the woman who stayed up until half 'not even coffee will help her wake up' in the morning." Nish glared over his shoulder at his sister. "She was muttering in French with her girlfriend."

"Does Vina know French?"

"Enough to make Amma blush." Nish dodged away from Vina when she lunged at him. "What? Am I wrong?"

"You are incredibly wrong." Vina straightened her stylish jumper. "He's been insufferable all day. Maybe someone switched his coffee for espresso."

"Is this what sex does to people?" Motts wrinkled her nose at the bubblier-than-normal Nish. She was glad at times like this to be asexual; she could enjoy romance without the dramatics and unnecessary noises. "Don't see the attraction."

The good-natured banter lasted until tea was poured, cakes were distributed, and seats had been found in the living room. Motts had retreated to an armchair with Cactus curled up beside her. Nish and River crowded into the other one, while Vina stretched out on the sofa like a princess on a chaise lounge.

Motts sipped her tea and pointedly avoided the not so subtle gazes sent her way. While she might not be brilliant at assessing body language or facial expression, the worry and sympathy was practically a living, breathing being in the room. She hated it.

"Have you messaged Teo?" River moved over to sit on the arm of her chair.

"He might be busy." Motts disliked being the first person to reach out—even via text, and even with family or Teo. "He's investigating. I've no doubt I'm on the list of people to talk to, since I found the body."

Again. Another body. I'm running quite a tally. Three dead bodies in one lifetime.

"Text him, Motts." River nudged her gently. "He'll be here before long and probably wonder why you didn't reach out to him when it happened."

"Will he?"

"Definitely," River promised.

"Are you sure? I wouldn't." Motts briefly met her cousin's gaze before turning her eyes back to Cactus, who purred contentedly. "Why?"

"It's a weird neurotypical thing. Just trust me. He'll worry if you don't text." River grabbed her mobile from the coffee table and handed it over. "Just say you're home safe with us. So he doesn't worry."

"Weirdly weird weirdness."

"I'm aware that we're odd." River snorted in amusement.

It was later in the evening when her friendly tormenters left the cottage. Motts chased them out with promises to text if she had nightmares. She wouldn't, but they'd be back in the morning to check on her.

They'd fallen into a similar routine after her near tumble off the cliff. Motts appreciated their concern. She did wish they'd trust her to reach out if it was necessary.

"I thought they'd never leave." Motts locked up behind them, turning on her security system. She'd used it religiously since Teo installed it for her. "Why don't I scrounge up your supper and a snack for myself? We can catch up on YouTube videos."

She had just set Cactus's bowl down when the doorbell rang. *Bugger.* Checking the front of the cottage via the app on her phone, Motts wasn't surprised to see Teo waiting patiently for her. He waved at the camera.

Motts left Cactus to his meal and went to open the door. "Did you identify the body?"

Teo ducked down to step through the doorway, squeezing by her to lift Cactus up when he trotted over to say hello. "Your welcome needs some work."

"Cactus handles the greeting. I pay him in catnip, tuna, and walks in the garden." Motts followed Teo and her cat through to the kitchen. He held Cactus comfortably in his arms while she went to fill up the kettle. "Well? Have you identified the victim?"

"Inspector Ash believes the victim is Nadine O'Connell, a kindly grandmother who'd been bedridden yet managed to go missing three years ago." Teo leaned against the counter, still petting Cactus gently. "They called me since I'm the nearest cold case detective."

"Not technically the nearest at the time."

"Ah, yes. The Londoner."

Motts set the kettle down and flicked it on, then peered over at him. "Why are you saying 'Londoner' like a curse word?"

"I'm not." Teo crossed his arms, dislodging an unhappy Cactus, who prowled away to finish his dinner. "What? I'm not."

"You definitely said Londoner like you meant wanker." Motts eyed the mountain of a detective inspector, taller than even Hugh. His brown eyes appeared tired, and his usual carefully coiffed greyish-black hair was mussed up. "The detective seemed nice enough to me."

"I'm sure he did."

Motts's frown deepened "You sound strange."

"I'm confident the London detective will be nothing but professional." Teo shrugged.

"*Right.*"

Chapter Three

MOTTS WOKE THE NEXT MORNING TO A CRICK IN HER neck, sunlight in her eyes, and an insistent paw poking at her cheek. "We've slept in."

Meow.

"Fine. I've slept in, and you've been kind enough to allow me the luxury." She plucked Cactus off her pillow and sat up slowly. "We've a garden to tend, a mystery to solve, and you need your morning walk."

Dragging herself out of bed, Motts took a quick warm shower. She changed into jeans and a light jumper, then headed into the kitchen with Cactus on her heels. After feeding both of her beloved creatures, she made a quick breakfast of lemon curd on toast with a large mug of tea.

They spent almost an hour in the garden. Cactus

chased after butterflies while Motts checked on her herbs and vegetable patches. She finally brought him inside and steeled her nerves to head down to the village.

Motts stepped out of the cottage to consider her two modes of transportation. She decided the day was warm enough not to take her Vespa and instead went with her 3-speed Pure City Step-Through in lovely seafoam green with dusty pink seats. Her customised bicycle shipped all the way from Los Angeles as a gift from her dad.

Placing her new origami flower bouquet samples along with her backpack into the saddlebags, Motts cycled down the hill into the village toward Marnie's bridal shop. She adored morning rides in Polperro before tourists swarmed the streets. Afternoons in the summer tended to get crowded.

"Oi! Watch out."

Motts swerved out of the way of an out-of-control hand trolley. She braked hard and watched it career down the road with a deliveryman chasing after. "Did I wake up in a Laurel and Hardy movie?"

"Sorry." Innis froze when he came around the side of a truck and spotted her. "Oh. It's you. O'Connell's delivery got away from him. He didn't aim for you."

"Didn't think he had."

Despite her best efforts, Innis and Rose Walters had maintained a stony distance from her. They hadn't forgiven Motts for her suspicions surrounding their involvement in his sister's death. Poor Rhona had been the person buried in her garden.

It didn't matter that they'd discovered the true killer—Rhona's boyfriend's best friend. Questions had already been asked. Rose had even gone so far as to vandalise the cottage.

Once the dust had settled, Motts hadn't been able to bridge the gap between them. A shame, since Innis and Rose ran the Salty Seaman, the best fish and chip shop in the area. She usually sent Vina or Nish in to get her order to avoid awkward small talk.

Motts sat on her bicycle, staring in Innis's general direction while he muttered to himself. "Right. Okay. Good morning, then."

"Motts, love. I've made a fresh pot of tea." Marnie stood outside of her shop, waving her over. She helped Motts lock up her bicycle, then carried in a few of the bouquets. "Aren't you clever? These will be perfect for my new window display for the summer brides."

"Thought you might like them." Motts shifted

uncomfortably. She didn't deal well with compliments, ever. "I brought a few sketches for other ideas."

"Brilliant. We'll have a tea and chat session." Marnie led her to the round table and chairs in the corner of the store where she met with brides. "And, you can tell me all about the handsome London copper my Perry keeps moaning about."

"Is he handsome?" Motts hadn't noticed. She did get a good feeling about Detective Inspector Byrne. He'd been there every step of the way while she faced her fears of the coastal path. "He'll make a nice friend."

"Friend?" Marnie chuckled.

"What?" Motts ignored the continued laughter from her friend. She carefully arranged the lily and wildflower paper bouquets on the table. "I've a few other ideas. I had the supplies to make these on hand so figured best to get you some for brides to see while I wait for my deliveries."

After getting her laughter under control, Marnie seemed content to stop teasing. Motts didn't understand why she'd found the London detective so amusing. Her non-autistic friends could be so confusing.

"You've got a visitor." Marnie nodded toward the

front of the shop. "Not the inspector I thought would track you down this morning."

Motts twisted in her chair to find Inspector Herceg stepping into the shop. The jaunty bell dinged cheerfully as the door opened. "Hello, Teo. How goes the investigating?"

He tucked his hands into pockets of his slightly rumpled suit jacket. "Slowly. As all cold cases tend to go. How are you ladies doing this morning?"

"My Perry mentioned it might be Mrs O'Connell. The poor dearie." Marnie stood up and went over to offer the inspector a cup of tea, which he declined. "I remember visiting with her. She'd gotten so ill. I thought maybe her family had taken her somewhere to get better care. Then they filed a missing person report after a few months. Poor woman."

Teo glanced from Marnie to Motts. "I'm sure we'll find out what happened."

"Why don't you two enjoy the weather?" Marnie gathered up the bouquets. "These are perfect. And we don't really need to chat about business anymore."

With impressive speed, Marnie ushered the two of them out of the store. Motts rolled her eyes in amusement. They'd been dating for over a month; they didn't need any help to spend time together.

"Why don't we grab a coffee at Griffin Brews?" Teo waited for Motts to secure her notebook in the saddlebag. He walked beside her while she pushed her bicycle along the street. "We can talk about our plans for the weekend, if you're still interested in coming to the knitting group."

In his spare time, the detective inspector enjoyed knitting. He regularly joined his mother's church group. Motts had gone to a few of the meetings, taking origami paper to craft since yarn bothered her fingers too much to muddle through a scarf or socks.

Or we can talk about Mrs O'Connell and why she looked as though she'd been killed two days ago yet has been missing for close to three years.

"Morning." Nish opened the door for her and Teo. He'd been cleaning the glass but looped his arm around hers to lead them toward the counter. "Amma is psychic. She claimed you'd be here and made chocolate, honey, and blackcurrant jam macarons especially for you. Lucky duck."

"Really?" Motts enjoyed most berries, but anything currant-flavoured held a special place in her heart. "Trust your mum to remember it's my favourite."

Nish gave her a hug, then went behind the

counter. "So, two coffees and a plate of treats for you both?"

"Are you going to let me pay for once?" Motts wasn't surprised when he waved off her and Teo's attempts. "Nish."

"Amma would never forgive me for charging her favourite child." Nish winked at her when she rolled her eyes in exasperation. "River's already eaten his weight in them."

"Thought they were for me?" Motts gestured to the variety of blackcurrant-themed pastries on offer. "You've all outdone yourselves. It's a week of Ribena."

"Ribena week. Don't let Vina hear you. She'll want to put out advertisements." Nish made their coffees perfectly. He handed one to her and the other to Teo. "I'll bring the plates over in a moment. Take your usual table in the corner."

Over their fancy coffees and macarons, Motts tried to probe Teo about the investigation. He skilfully avoided answering her questions directly. She didn't think her attempt at subtlety was working.

"Motts." Teo stopped stirring his coffee and focused his attention fully on her. "I can't give you any details about the investigation. Haven't you had your fill of being close to a murder victim?"

"I found her. Unnamed, unknown, uncovered." Motts hated running out of words before completing an alliteration. "Bodies decompose in the sea, don't they? How'd she wind up looking a few days dead?"

"Motts."

"Mottsy," Vina called out to her from across the café, waving her over. "*Motts*."

"Persistent Pravina persists passionately. Better." Motts slipped out of her chair and met Vina by the counter. "What?"

"Silver fox at ten o'clock," Vina whispered.

Motts checked the time on the clock behind her. "It's not ten."

"Of all the...." Vina trailed off, shaking her head. "There's a silver fox approaching."

"There aren't any silver foxes in Polperro. Maybe you should call animal control?" Motts glanced at Vina, who raised a hand up to cover her face. "What is it?"

"Ms Mottley?"

She twisted around to the London detective approaching. "Motts, Inspector. Everyone calls me Motts aside from my mother. Are you here for coffee?"

Vina groaned loudly into her hand. "Silver. Fox."

"DI Byrne." Teo strode across the café with his

hand outstretched. "Thought you'd headed back to London?"

"Cold cases are my area of expertise. Ms Mottley has kindly agreed to help with the case involving her childhood friend. And since I'm in Cornwall, I may as well offer my assistance to the local detectives." Inspector Byrne took Teo's hand. "Perry Ash filled me in on the details."

"Did he?"

"What are they doing?" Motts whispered to Vina and Nish, who were still behind the counter. The two detectives were having the longest handshake she'd ever seen. Neither of them had stepped back. "Is this some weird police ritual?"

"It's not a copper thing." Vina snickered.

"What does that even mean?" Motts frowned at her ex-girlfriend. "Why are neurotypicals so strange?"

Nish patted her shoulder. "They're communicating."

"*Right.*" Motts decided she didn't care what they meant.

Chapter Four

"I FANCY ICE CREAM." MOTTS HAD FINISHED HER morning routine. Breakfast? Check. Fed and walked the little creatures? Done. Responded to emails after hiding from them? Mostly accomplished. She made sure both her cat and turtle were set up for being home alone. "Don't let any stray felines into the house. I'm trusting you to keep Moss safe."

Gathering up her bag and the small camera her uncle Tomato had gotten for her as a present, Motts decided to trek down to Talland Bay. The small beach on the west tended to be quiet even in the middle of a busy Cornish summer.

I'll have to thank the London inspector. I needed a little push to get me out of the cottage and exploring again. Maybe he'll be able to solve Jenny's murder after all.

The weather had cooled slightly even with the bright sunlight. Motts opted for the shorter route along Bridals Lane. It wouldn't do for cycling, not on her bike; too many slippery rocks to traverse.

Changing out of her trainers into a sturdier hiking shoe, Motts headed outside. She'd texted River to invite him to meet her in Talland Bay in two hours. Her cousin always enjoyed skiving off work for a visit to the beach, and Motts figured that after a dip of her toes in the water, she could indulge in a lovely ice cream from the nearby café. She locked up the cottage and took obsessive care in setting the security system. Cactus and Moss mattered more to her than anything.

She made her way up Talland Hill to Bridals Lane. The picturesque hedge-lined single-lane road tapered down to a trail, veering off to the right. She went slowly to avoid slipping.

The foliage rose up on either side of the lane. It was lush, green, and almost claustrophobic. Trees towered above her, blocking the sun from practically blinding her.

Dodging the trickle of water flowing down the

middle of the lane, Motts continued down before emerging out at Talland Bay. She took a moment to breathe in the salty sea air while the wind blew her hair wildly behind her. It had definitely been worth the hour-long walk.

She grabbed a cup of tea from the Talland Bay Beach Café, promising herself an ice cream for the trip home. One lone couple sat on the sand to the far left of the beach. She made her way along the right to clamber up on some rocks to sit and watch the slowly rising tide.

After finishing up her tea, Motts clambered off the rocks. The tide was beginning to inch too close for comfort. She had no intentions of going for a swim.

Returning to the café, Motts ordered a brie and cranberry panini. She got a top-up of her tea as well. One of the small sheds with picnic tables to the side of the restaurant was free, so she slipped inside to enjoy her sandwich in peace.

"Hello, yon tiny Pineapple." Her uncle gave a dramatic flourish of a bow. He enjoyed acting as though life were a stage for him. "Enjoying the sea?"

"Uncle Tomato." Motts peered around, but her cousin was nowhere to be seen. "Is River okay?"

"His mum insisted on his helping her at the brewery." He sat across from at her. "Have you had an ice cream yet?"

Tom Mottley was her dad's younger brother. He ran Chen-Mottley brewery with his wife, Lily, and their son, River; they lived next door to her grand-parents. Her uncle and auntie had met in Singapore while students and fallen in love. She'd called him Uncle Tomato for as long as she could remember.

"River showed me your text message, and I never turn down good ice cream." He gave her a broad smile. "He couldn't tell his mum no."

"Only child problems." Motts knew all about dealing with a full force of parental interest with no distractions. "Shouldn't you be working?"

"I am working. Dessert beer?"

Motts frowned at her uncle, trying to decipher if he was teasing her. She feigned a chuckle just in case it was a joke. Better to laugh than have him staring at her for not doing so. "Sounds vile."

"Only teasing, love." He reached across the table to pat her hand. "Why don't we grab our ice creams and walk along the beach? Then I can give you a lift home while you tell me all about this new mystery you've discovered."

"Who told?"

"It's Cornwall, tiny Pineapple. A woman floating in the sea makes the news no matter how quiet the police try to keep it." He winked at her and smiled, reminding her of her dad for a moment. "Well? Are you putting out your detective shingle? Your gran will be so proud. You know her and your granddad are wondering when you'll come round next."

"Uncle Tomato," Motts groaned. "I'm not going to be a private detective."

"Might be fun."

"Dead bodies aren't fun." She took the last bite of her sandwich. "Teo and Perry are the detectives."

"Tell you what. Ice cream. Home. And I'll have plenty of time to convince you how capable and brilliant you are." He tapped her chin when she turned away toward the sea. "Okay. I'll stop embarrassing you. What flavour treat are you having?"

"They've got in a new flavour from Roskilly's. Cream Tea Ice Cream." Motts gathered up the remnants from her early lunch. "They also have toffee and hazelnut, your favourite."

After procuring their ice cream, they strolled along the beach. Motts grew increasingly uneasy as more people came to enjoy the sunshine and sea breezes. Her uncle looped his arm around her shoulders to guide her toward his car; she got in, and thankfully he let her doze in silence the entire way home to Polperro.

"Oh, I almost forgot." He slowed to a stop outside of her cottage. He reached into the back to grab a Tupperware container. "Your auntie made biscuits for you. The lemon-ginger spiced ones. And my River wanted to remind you about the YouTube night?"

Motts had to laugh at the slightly confused tone to her uncle's voice. "I don't watch telly, so we have a playlist of YouTube videos that we watch instead of having a movie night."

"Kids these days."

"You were drinking beer behind the pub and stealing fish from the market. I think eating snacks and watching videos is mild in comparison." She clutched the container of biscuits to her chest. "Drive safely, Uncle Tomato."

"Enjoy your biscuits. Better hide them, or River and Nish will eat the lot." He gave her an awkward hug in the vehicle. "Off you go. There's a special one in there for Cactus as well."

Watching her uncle drive off, Motts finally

turned around to head into the cottage. She checked to make sure Monty, her bicycle, was still secured by the side of the house. *I'm going to need to tidy the front garden at some point. It's a bit of a mess.*

"Hello, Cactus." Motts found him sitting on the little table by the front door waiting for her. "Did you enjoy your morning?"

Meow.

"I had a lovely walk." Motts wandered through the living room to check on Moss. "I found a new rock on the beach for you. Here. What do you think?"

Meow.

"I didn't forget you." Motts retrieved the crumpled-up paper she'd gotten at the café. She tossed it on the floor. "Pounce away. And a little tomato told me that there's a treat for you in this container."

With a happy chirp, Cactus chased the paper along the wooden floor. Motts watched him play for several minutes. The siren call of chai drew her into the kitchen.

Taara Khatri, Vina's current girlfriend, had travelled recently to Lahore from London for business and had brought a special brand of ginger and cardamom chai back with her. Motts had already drunk her way through half of the tea. She hoped Taara made another trip soon.

Waiting for the electric kettle to heat up, Motts explored the contents of her fridge. YouTube night meant snacks. Lots of them. The twins would scavenge around the bakery; River would probably grab something from his mum's after work.

Boys.

The evening always happened at Motts's cottage because she could relax. They'd attempted to gather at Nish and River's place, but she'd left within an hour. Lesson learned.

With a cup of chai and a few ginger biscuits, Motts got settled at her kitchen table to work. She'd been commissioned to make a quilled violin for a birthday present. Quilling always helped her relax; something about gently arranging scrolled slips of paper into beautiful art eased the tension in her soul.

From her original sketch, Motts had lined out the violin itself with a stark white paper. She filled in the empty space in the shadow box with a series of scrolled filigree in shades of brown and gold. All she had left was to finish up the last few details.

Her doorbell rang several hours later. Motts carefully closed the shadow box on her finished art. It wouldn't do for Cactus to ruin it now, the mischievous feline.

"Amma made medhu vadai for us." Vina squeezed by Motts into the cottage when she opened the door. Nish and River followed after her. "Loads of them. They're still crispy, fresh from the fryer."

"She wouldn't let us steal any of the fritters," River complained. He gave Motts a quick hug. "Mum had these steamed pork baos hanging around. I grabbed a few."

"He grabbed all of them. Pretty sure your auntie's going to have words with us." Nish carried a paper bag of his own. "Nothing as fancy from me. I picked up my weight in chips from the Salty Seaman. Innis might be a grumpy bastard, but he makes the best fried, greasy potato strips of joy in Cornwall."

Three hours later, the boys had headed home, taking all the leftover food. Motts and Vina sat in relative silence. They'd watched a playlist of funny videos from both the React and Try channels.

Vina was stretched out on the sofa with her head resting on a cushion. "Just us girls."

"And Cactus."

"Sorry, Cactus." Vina nudged the cat sleeping by her feet. "Us girls and a succulent."

"And Moss."

"Mustn't forget the turtle," Vina teased. "Can I continue?"

"I don't know."

Vina dropped her head against the couch. "Pineapple Meg Mottley. Must you be so literal and pedantic?"

"Yes," she answered truthfully.

"What do you say we crash a funeral?" Vina got straight to the point instead of teasing her further. "Marnie heard from Peggy Shine at her shop who spoke with one of the O'Connells. The family are having a small service at the church in the morning. Not sure it's a burial; I think they're just having a celebration of life or whatever it's called."

"And?"

"We could go. Meet the family. Ask a few subtle questions about their poor departed Nan." Vina completely ignored Motts when she began to shake her head emphatically. "Aren't you curious to know how she wound up in the sea?"

"More curious to why she seemed only hours dead. How, if she went missing years ago?" Motts admitted. "And why now?"

"Both excellent questions." Vina sat up and leaned forward with her elbows resting on her legs. "Marnie's going. I can put together a little box of treats from the café. We can be concerned neighbours."

"Nosy neighbours."

"We live in a tiny village." Vina grinned at her. "All neighbours are nosy."

Chapter Five

"Ready?" Vina had strong-armed Motts out of her cottage into a car early the next morning. The drive to the church hadn't taken long; short enough they could've walked, but Vina hadn't wanted to risk ruining her dress. "We're presentable enough."

"For what?" Motts tried to pry Vina's fingers off her arm. "Where's Marnie?"

"Last-minute appointment with a panicky bride." Vina steered her through the gate toward the doors. "Hurry. We don't want to be late. We might miss something important."

"I can't do this." Motts jerked away from Vina and fled around the opposite side of the building. She ducked behind a stone sign when two angry, arguing men blocked her path. "I want to be at home."

Who argues at a funeral?

"Please don't make a scene, Jasper. Think about Mum." The younger of the two men seemed to be trying to calm the other down. They were dressed for the funeral, appearing to be in their twenties. "She won't want to see her sons arguing while we're burying Gran."

"Think about Mum? Bit rich. When the bloody hell has she thought about us? Sod off, Mikey." Jasper shoved his brother against the wall of the church. "Why don't you be a good boy and leave me alone?"

"Let's just get through this circus, and you can go back to pretending I don't exist." Mikey stomped by his brother, who followed him.

After waiting a few seconds to ensure they'd gone, Motts snuck away from the church. She made her way through the village and climbed wearily up the narrow staircase that led up the hill to her street. Vina knew her well enough to not follow.

"Motts?"

She paused on the last step and contemplated rolling back down the staircase. "No."

"Miss Mottley?" Detective Inspector Byrne

sounded concerned and confused. She didn't have the energy to glance up at him.

"No." Motts slipped by him into the cottage and closed the door. She slid to the floor, sitting with her back against the solid wood. "No."

What did River say about breathing?

Why do I always panic like this?

Right. Breathe in. One, two, three, four, five. Out. One, two, three, four, five. I can do this. I can.

Riding out the intense energy from a meltdown, Motts rubbed her arms roughly, trying to stop the odd sensation of electricity under her skin. *Just keep breathing.* Cactus sidled up next to her. He curled up in her lap, offering comfort.

Over an hour later, a knock jolted her out of her doze on the floor. Motts got slowly to her feet, trying to ease the kinks out of her legs. She opened the door to find no one on the other side.

"Hello?" She peered around and saw no one, but found a larger paper cup and a cloth-covered basket on her doorstep. "What?"

Taking the lid off the cup, Motts sniffed cautiously and recognised the scent of Nish's special spiced café mocha. He made it especially for her, usually on days when she'd had a meltdown. How had he known?

Motts carried the basket and coffee into the cottage. She kicked the door shut behind her once Cactus had raced down the hall. "Maybe we'll find a treat for you as well?"

Meow.

Underneath the cloth napkin, Motts found a note in Nish's neat handwriting. *Had a few words with Vina about pushing you when she knows she shouldn't. The silver fox of a detective from London came around to see if I could help. He also text messaged Teo. Can you believe it? I'll come round later with River to check on you. Remember to breathe.*

Setting the note to one side, Motts found a selection of what was clearly the café's baked offerings for the day. She sank down on one of the kitchen chairs, drawing her legs up underneath her. It had been a while since anxiety had gotten the best of her.

She wondered what Teo's response would be. He'd been a little distant in the past few weeks. She'd decided not to let it worry her; detectives had a lot on their plate.

She had no doubts the exhaustion that always followed a meltdown would kick in soon. Nish knew her well enough to have provided food requiring no effort on her part. She grabbed a curry-spiced chocolate croissant and her coffee, deciding to enjoy the lovely gesture.

Cactus leapt up on the table and inched over to her. He stretched out on his back, staring up at her with curious eyes. Motts dug into the basket to find a cat-friendly treat; she came out triumphantly with a little tuna roll made specifically for him.

"I knew they wouldn't forget." She set the treat down for him. "Off you go. Show your prize to Moss."

Her cat and turtle had a great affinity for each other. Motts was convinced they gossiped together. Cactus certainly spent a massive amount of time beside Moss's terrarium.

With her coffee and croissant, Motts wandered into the living room. She curled up on the sofa under her weighted blanket. The wind had picked up, so she allowed her mind to settle while watching clouds drift across the blue Cornish sky.

One of the advantages of having moved to Cornwall over living in London was her mother no longer smothered her with care. If Motts had a bad day, she had the time and space to recover. She'd discovered retreating into the solitude of her cottage did wonders.

Motts came out of her daze by late afternoon.

She'd ignored the beeping of her phone signalling text messages. If it was a real emergency, they'd call.

They'll call. I'll ignore it, but at least I'll know to check my messages.

Content to continue watching the garden through the window, Motts didn't move until after the sun had set. She got up when someone knocked on the door. *I'm surprised Vina stayed away this long. I suppose I'll have to deal with the drama now.*

"You're not Vina." Motts stared at Detective Inspector Teo Herceg. "Much taller, definitely grumpier."

"I'm not grumpy. Stoic is a better word."

"Right."

"I've been sent with supper from Leena Griffin. She insisted." Teo lifted a paper sack. "She reminded me of my own mother. A commanding presence in a petite body."

"Pretty sure it's a mum thing." Motts grabbed the bag and led the inspector into her cottage. "Have you eaten?"

"I could eat." Teo seemed to be inspecting her while she moved around the kitchen getting plates.

"Inspector inspects intensely," Motts muttered. She shifted uncomfortably under his concerned gaze. "What is it?"

"You ran away from a funeral. Want to talk about it?"

"Not particularly." She eased open the multiple containers of food. "Oh, paruppu sadam with potato curry, uttapam, and sambhar."

"Smells delicious."

Motts pointed to the paruppu sadam. "That's spiced rice which goes with the curry. The uttapam is the fried pizza-like dish made of rice and lentils that you dip into the red lentil sambhar."

It seemed Amma Griffin believed her daughter owed an apology, and food obviously made for the best *mea culpa*. Motts would have to pay the café a visit in the morning.

Sorting out the Tamil-themed feast onto two plates, Motts led the way into the living room. They got comfortable on the sofa. She put on a jazz playlist on Spotify, one she knew Teo would appreciate.

"I see this wasn't your first gift of food." Teo nodded toward the basket from earlier in the day. "Wondered if he actually delivered it."

"Why did he do this?" Motts nudged Teo with her foot. He reached down to cover it with his hand. "And why did you help him?"

"I get the idea DI Byrne has become emotionally

impacted by a series of cold cases connected to Jenny's. As she was your closest friend, I imagine he's taken an interest in you." Teo squeezed her foot gently. "And I helped you. Not him."

"You two seemed at odds before." Motts still didn't quite understand their strange behaviour at the café earlier in the week. She waved her hand to stop him when Teo went to speak. "Doesn't matter. I think he wants to be friends."

Teo rubbed his thumb across the top of her foot, then lifted his hand away. "I'm sure he does. What were you doing at the funeral anyway? I wasn't aware you knew the O'Connells."

"I don't." Motts shredded a piece of the uttapam in her fingers. She plucked a sliver of fried onion from the remnants. "Do you know how she died?"

"Motts." He stared sternly down at her. "Haven't you been close enough to the investigation?"

"Only curious." Motts tossed the onion into her mouth. "We haven't talked in a while."

"The chief inspector's had a push for me to wrap up cases of late."

"Okay." Motts grabbed her mug. "Can you rush solving a case?"

"No."

Chapter Six

MEOW.

"What have I said about interrupting work?" Motts lifted Cactus carefully out from her pile of peonies. She'd spent the morning folding flowers for a bride-to-be. Marnie needed the bouquet within the next few days. "You aren't allowed to play with the origami."

Meow.

"Fine. I'll make you a paper mouse." Motts snagged a spare scrap to fold a creature for him. "You are spoiled."

Meow.

"Don't get testy with me. I've already fed you extra tuna, plus you're wearing the soft jumper Teo knitted for you." She still found it adorably amusing how the large and muscular detective inspector who brooded with the best of them spent his free time knitting with a group of grandmothers. "Don't frown at me."

The jumper had been for the winter, but even on summer days Cactus sometimes had to wear a jumper. Despite being a "hairless" cat, he had what amounted to peach fuzz for fur. Motts had to keep him warm to keep him from falling ill.

Meow.

"Patience is a virtue." Motts finished with the last fold. She flicked the mouse along the table, chuckling when Cactus leapt after it. "Funny feline frolics fiercely."

Turning her attention to the flowers, Motts finished the last six. She gathered the peonies and gently added prepared stems, which she'd made out of wire wrapped with paper. The arranging of an origami bouquet was often the most challenging part. She had to ensure nothing got crushed or bent.

Paper flower bouquets might last longer than real ones, but they tended to be more prone to breaking. Motts finished with her creation and placed it carefully into a hatbox. She'd found them to be the perfect size, and they fit on the back of her Vespa.

Meow.

"Yes, you are the slayer of the paper monster." Motts surveyed the remnants of the origami mouse. "Were you a dog in a past life?"

Meow.

"I apologise for the insult." Motts lifted Cactus up into her arms, snuggling him against her chest. "I'm heading into the village. Can you protect the cottage and Moss for me?"

Setting him down, Motts made sure the hatbox lid was securely fastened. She didn't want to waste her hours of work on one reckless turn. Marnie would be pleased to have the bouquet a day early.

She glanced at the time on her phone. It was too early for lunch. *Maybe I can ride along the coast.*

No, no. Stop it.

I am not going to involve myself in this investigation.

Motts debated with herself all the way down to the village. She was still grumbling to herself when she plopped the hatbox down on the counter in front of Marnie. "Here."

"Wake up on the wrong side of the morning, did we?" Marnie teased.

Right.

Polite small talk.

"Sorry." Motts sometimes forgot about the intricacies of neurotypical communication. "I was rude."

"Only a little." Marnie waved off her apology with a kind smile. "What's in the box?"

"The peony bouquet."

"Excellent." Marnie peeked inside, then set the box aside. She leaned forward with her elbows on the counter. "You'll never guess what I've learned."

"Marnie." Motts was amused at how everyone around her, aside from the policemen in her life, seemed determined to turn her into an amateur detective. "What have you learned?"

"Apparently, poor Mrs O'Connell died three years ago. Stabbed with something, they don't know what. And my Perry believes she was kept in a freezer, which explains the state of her body." Marnie kept her voice low and her eyes on the front of the shop. "A freezer. Can you imagine?"

"I'm trying not to." Motts tried to resist the curiosity building up in her. Marnie's gossip had only added fuel to the flames of the mystery. "Why would someone throw the body into the sea now?"

"Maybe someone got too close to discovering her?" She shrugged. "My Perry says the 'fancy detectives' have taken over the investigation."

"Perry knows Teo. They watch football together."

"He enjoys taking the mickey." Marnie shifted the hatbox further down the counter. She glanced at Motts's confused face. "Men, people really, often enjoy poking at each other even when they don't mean it."

"Right." Motts understood sarcasm more than other types of humour. Teasing and pranks, though, never made much sense to her. "I should get going. Any more orders for me?"

"I'll email you. I've a few possible ones but nothing concrete." Marnie considered her for a moment. "I won't hug you this morning. You seem to be enjoying your little bubble too much."

With a friendly wave, Motts headed out of the shop. She stopped once outside to inhale deeply. The summer sun was obscured by a fluffy cloud, allowing her to enjoy the blue skies and relatively calm breeze coming off the sea through the village.

Motts stood by her Vespa parked in front of the bridal shop. *How do I go about learning about tides and currents around Polperro? The killer clearly hasn't dragged the body along the coastal path. So, where did they dump the poor departed grandmother?*

Stop it.

I'm not investigating. I'm not. Well, maybe a few questions.

Just a few maritime queries. A little knowledge never hurt anyone. I live by the sea; perfectly normal to want to know about the sea.

"Out of my way, you stupid bint."

Motts turned all the way around, looking at the distance between herself and the grumpy seventy-something-year-old man glaring at her. "I'm not in your way."

"Cheeky youths." Mr Orchard, the elder, still held a grudge for her suspecting his grandson of murder. He'd once been her auntie's gardener, but his fondness hadn't transferred to Motts one iota. "Loitering around. Lurking like a proper criminal."

"I'm almost forty." She blinked at the crotchety pensioner. "Not loitering. Not cheeky. Also, not a youth."

"Always poking your nose."

"Always?" Motts bristled at the accusation.

"Not bothering my friend, are you?" Marnie stepped out of the shop. "Go on, Motts. Mr Orchard and I can chat about lace."

Lace?

While Mr Orchard seemed as confused as Motts at the suggestion, she took her bid for freedom. Marnie could handle the grumpy gardener. *Cheeky youth, indeed.*

Now what? Who can I ask about sea currents and tides? It seemed like random knowledge Teo might collect, but he'd know why she was asking.

Rounding a corner, Motts spotted the Polperro post office. *Doc.* Carridoc and Elys Ferris had run the local branch for years. She knew the elderly couple had a keen interest in Cornish history but also in the fishing industry.

Anyone who knows about the fishing industry surely understands the local currents a little?

Can you google currents?

It wasn't as though Motts needed an in-depth understanding. She wanted to figure out where the body would likely have been dumped. The killer might've left evidence behind.

Maybe I'm not as resistant to putting my nose in as I claimed.

"Hello, love. Package to mail?" Elyse waved cheerily when Motts stepped into the post office. "Don't think we've got anything for you."

"No packages." Motts shook her head. "I wanted to learn about the currents and tides around Polperro."

"Currents in the sea?" Doc popped up from behind the counter. "Not sure I can help. You might chat with young Callie who runs the kayak shop.

She does guided trips from Fowey to Looe, going by our fair village. She'd know about the seas around the coast."

Am I curious enough to chat with a complete stranger?

Bugger.

Chapter Seven

"You keep Moss and yourself safe. I'll be home before tea." Motts had spent most of the previous day practising her questions for Callie in the mirror before writing them down. She didn't feel confident, but her curiosity was pushing her forward. "I can do this, right?"

With a meow of confidence from Cactus, Motts finished checking the windows and doors. She headed outside, making sure to set the alarm system behind her. It was a beautiful morning for a ride.

Poor Monty.

He deserves better than being restricted to the village.

"Are you ready, Monty?" Motts patted her bicycle before storing her water bottle and backpack into the saddlebags. "Fowey or bust."

She knew from past cycling trips that the journey would take an hour or so depending on whether she chose to stop along the way. Given the stunningly gorgeous weather, she fully intended to take her time. Doc had assured her that Callie planned to be in the shop all day.

Deciding to cycle straight to Fowey, Motts had promised herself a few saffron buns and two jars of ginger honey from the Quay Bakery. She also intended to enjoy a stroll to Lantic Bay on the way home. It would do her good to stretch her legs along the beach.

The route from Polperro to Polruan where Motts would catch the ferry went along narrow lanes with high hedgerows on both sides. She had to dodge a few vehicles on the way, but mostly had the roads to herself. It felt good to be out in the sunshine.

Her journey ended far too quickly for her nerves. Motts found the ferry gave her more than enough time to panic. She wanted answers, though, and made herself walk the short distance from the Whitehouse Quay to Callie's Kayaks.

"Can I help you?"

Motts didn't know what she'd expected when she met Callie. It wasn't the slim, muscular brunette with her short hair perfectly sculpted into a wavy sort of Mohawk. "Brilliant hairstyle."

"Thanks." Callie grinned. "You must be Motts."

"Pineapple Mottley. Prefer Motts," she admitted with an awkward smile. "Did Doc mention me?"

"Called last night. My wife's out leading a guided kayak tour around the coast." Callie waved her over to the counter. "He said you wanted to know about the currents. Any particular reason?"

"I...." Motts hesitated. She didn't quite know how to explain without sounding as though she'd lost the plot. "I'm not a kayaker."

"My mate used to hike around Polperro quite a bit until he ran into some angry woman who accused him of being a thief. He had a devil of a time convincing the police of his innocence. Bad enough he lived out of his backpack." She grabbed a bottle of water and took a long drink. "Ashby. Posh, I know. His family bunged him out for not conforming. He stays with us when he's not trekking around Cornwall and camping. We know waters from here to Looe like the backs of our hands."

"Did you hear about the body found in the sea by the lighthouse?" Motts pressed her lips together to stop groaning audibly. *Way to ease the question into the conversation. Subtle.* "I'm surprised no one saw the perpetrator carrying a body along the coastal path."

"Not so surprising. I'd wager they dumped the body further down." Callie reached underneath the counter and placed a chart of Cornwall between them. "See these lines around the coast. You drop anything from the Polperro docks or anywhere west of the village, I'd bet my kayak it would drift around and wind up caught on those rocks during high tide."

"Really?"

"Definitely. I don't even need my charts to tell you. My wife did a study during university for her master's. We had to experiment with floating on the currents. I almost wrecked my best kayak in the process." Callie reached under the counter again and came up with a pamphlet. "I'll circle a few spots on the map. If I'd done it, I'd have dumped the poor woman somewhere between there and the docks. These would be the easiest to get to."

"Oh?"

"Actually." She tapped her finger against the map. "They went out in a boat. Had to have. I'd bet you my whole shop whoever did this went out in a boat and expected the body to either sink or drift out to sea."

"Makes more sense than them rolling her off a cliff." Motts spotted a mobile of origami boats in the corner of the shop. "I made those for a wedding bouquet. I'd never made one out of kayaks."

"So you're Marnie's supplier." Callie's ever-present smile grew even wider. "She wouldn't tell us."

Motts lifted a hand to wave. "That would be me. Marnie's better at the talking bit."

She tilted her head to one side. "Think you did fine."

Motts scratched the back of her neck. She took the folded up map. "Thanks for this."

"If you want to kayak around the area, give us a call. I'm up for a mystery." Callie handed her a card with their numbers. "Tell Doc he owes me a pint at the pub next time I'm in Polperro."

They chatted further about Callie's thoughts on the killer going out in a boat, which surprised Motts, since conversing with strangers didn't usually come naturally to her. She even offered to take her out in a kayak for a fresh perspective. Motts wasn't quite ready to play Captain Blight yet.

Seasick sailors sail sparingly.

Sparingly?

I don't even make sense in my own thoughts.

Leaving the shop, Motts headed further into Fowey. Quay Bakery on Fore Street was a short cycle away. She came away with a bag of saffron buns along with a jar of ginger honey.

The siren call of sugar forced her to stop at the Fowey Sweet Shop. Motts stocked up on Kernow chocolates. She'd eaten the mountain of lemon meringue and white chocolate bars Teo had given her a few months ago.

Buoyed by the scents of baked goods and sweets, Motts grabbed a drink before heading to the ferry. She had enough time on the trip across to Polruan to finish a bun and the hot tea. Her earbuds helped her avoid casual conversation; tourists, in general, enjoyed being chatty.

Motts did not.

On the journey home, Motts opted not to detour to Lantic Bay. She'd had enough of people for one day. Her visit to Fowey had taken longer than she'd intended.

It would be better to visit the few areas Callie suggested early in the morning—fewer people to deal with. Despite the tea and bun, Motts's tummy grumbled at her by the time she cycled through the village. She wanted fish and chips, but Innis always glared at her when she went to the Salty Seaman.

I know I accused him of murdering his sister, but I did apologise.

"Need a hand?"

Motts started in surprise and glanced over to find Nish wiping his hands off on his apron beside her. "Where'd you come from?"

"Amma saw you out the window of the café. Wanting fish and chips?" He nodded his head toward the Salty Seaman. "Want me to get your lunch for you?"

"He shouts with his eyes," Motts muttered defensively.

"Shouts with his mouth as well." Nish pulled off his apron and draped it across the basket on her bicycle. "Double portion so Cactus can steal from your lunch?"

"I'll pay you in honey." Motts retrieved the extra jar she'd gotten. "Thought you might enjoy experimenting with baking."

"Amma makes the best honey cake. This would be brilliant. I'll bring some over later." Nish glanced down the street. "I'll be back in a moment."

Motts tried not to stare at the fish shop. She saw Nish and the grumpy Innis talking. "Interesting."

Nish returned a few minutes later. "Innis apparently saw you as well. Had the meal prepped before I even asked."

"Shouty eyes."

"He of the shouty eyes had your food ready and refused to take my fiver." Nish placed the packet into her basket, grabbed the jar of honey, and gave her a quick hug. "Off home with you. I'll keep Vina from bothering you this evening."

Motts appreciated how Nish never pushed her for more. "Give her a hug for me."

"Your version or mine?"

"Whichever." Motts shrugged. "Don't get into it with your sister. I don't want your amma calling to complain."

"As if she'd complain to her favourite child about us." Nish nudged her. "Only teasing."

The rest of the afternoon went by in a pleasantly quiet blur. Motts ate her lunch in the garden with Cactus. They'd lazed in the sun until angry voices on the other side of the garden fence chased them inside.

Someone had been walking along the path on the coastal side of her garden, having a massive row. Motts was almost curious enough to poke her head over the fence. She wondered if Teo would add an additional camera for her.

Maybe I shouldn't be too nosy.

Deciding the day called for a hot chocolate, Motts wandered into the kitchen. She set a pot on the stove and mixed milk, double cream, chocolate, and a hint of coffee. The latter being her dad's secret ingredient.

Meow.

"Yes, they were rude to disturb your afternoon walk." Motts grabbed one of the treats from the counter and offered it to Cactus. "How about we snuggle in by the window and read about kayaking in Cornwall?"

Meow.

"I'll remember to turn the security system on. Just in case."

Chapter Eight

"Since when is there an island off Polperro?" Motts brushed her hair out of her eyes and bent forward to inspect the map more closely. "Ah. Toast crumb. Not an isle so much as a refuge of buttered bread abandoned in your haste to steal my breakfast."

Buttered bread bounces beyond borders.

And now I'm hungry again.

A second round of lemon curd on buttered toast soothed her renewed hunger. Motts had woken up early. She wanted to meander around the docks after the fishing vessels had gone out but before the rest of the world was up and about.

Plus, Nish had texted last night. His mum had a

ginger honey cake for her. Motts never turned down Leena's creations.

"I'll bring a treat home for you. I promise." Motts bent down to rub Cactus's head when he followed her to the front door. "You had your walk already. And even this early, I wouldn't risk someone running off with you. Or you going off trying to hunt down a fish of your own. Greedy guts."

Cactus retreated into the cottage with a flick of his tail. He was probably going to complain to Moss about her cruelty. With a smile, Motts headed outside, making sure to lock up carefully.

She cycled down the hill to the village. With summer came the closing of local streets to vehicles; the narrow lanes of Polperro didn't lend way to increased traffic. But she didn't really have to worry about tourists at half-past six.

No one was so interested in a quaint fishing village to get up with the sun.

Her evening had been spent reading up on tides and the Polperro port. Motts had a suspicion whoever dumped the body had gone out from there. If so, according to her research, they'd have a six-hour window, three on either side of the high tide, to push off from the village.

A tricky thing to manage, since high tide the day

they'd found the body would've been around three in the morning. *Probably not a coincidence.* Not many people out and about so early. She wondered if CCTV cameras around the harbour had caught anything.

Motts made her way slowly through the quiet village. She noticed the van from the cold storage facility located on the quayside where a lot of the fish wound up that wasn't immediately taken by commercial buyers or the local fish market. *I hope he minds his trolley this morning; I'm not awake enough to play dodge the projectile.*

Riding up to the harbour, Motts locked her bicycle up against one of the railings. She strolled along the right side of the docks. Most of the fishing trawlers had already made their way out to sea; they'd be gone for a few days if the weather held.

Motts carefully went down the stairs leading directly to the water. The tide had pulled out, leaving a small area to step without going for a dip in the sea. She peered around, trying to see any sort of sign.

What am I looking for? There are loads of boats in and out of the harbour. Even if I find something, there's no guarantee it's related to poor old Mrs O'Connell.

A glint of light caught her attention on her way

up the stairs. Motts crouched down to find a scrap of fabric from a coat along with a distinctive toggle type of button. She grabbed her phone and took several photos before gently tugging it out from between the jagged stones along the wall.

Motts considered her options and sent a text with one of the images to Teo. "I can always claim to have accidentally stumbled on it during a morning walk. By docks. Where it's slippery and stinks of briny fish."

Giving the entire side of the harbour a more thorough glance, Motts didn't find any other potential clues. She hadn't received a response from Teo but sent a follow-up text inviting him to coffee at the café. He'd stayed with his parents in Looe, since the cold case would keep him close to Polperro.

She knocked on the side door to the café and secured her bicycle to a nearby lamppost while waiting. "Morning."

"Come in for a mug of coffee and some cake." Leena swung the door open and waved her inside. "I've got the ovens going full blast. We're trying some new summer pasties and macarons this morning."

"No minions doing your bidding?"

"My babies are elbow-deep in flour at the

moment." Leena looped her arm around Motts. "What has you up so early?"

"Your babies are in their thirties." Motts allowed herself to be led through the dimly lit café into the kitchen. "Something smells divine."

"Amma had the idea to play around with rose-flavoured custard. We're hoping for bright, summery macarons. Made a few mango cream ones as well." Vina brushed her flour-covered hands off on her brother's shirt, ignoring his indignant shout. "Does Cactus approve of you being out this early?"

"I imagine he's commiserating with Moss as we speak." Motts sidled over to Nish, who'd managed to clean his shirt off. "You mentioned ginger honey cake."

"Glad you're happy to see us." He nudged her with his elbow.

"If you give me honey cake, I'll show you the clue I found by the harbour." Motts stared him down— well, at his nose more than his eyes. He blinked first. "Cake, coffee, clues, carefully considered contem-plation."

"Eight out of ten." Vina scored her alliteration.

"Nine. Cake deserves an extra point," Nish argued.

While Leena lightly scolded her children, who

laughed in response, Motts happily accepted the slice of sticky honey cake Nish offered. They moved away from the baking zone into a small table in the corner. The Griffins usually had their lunches there.

"What's the clue?" Vina had the least amount of patience of the twins. She set three mugs of coffee on the table and slipped into the chair beside Motts. "Well?"

Motts eased the fabric out of her pocket and set it on the table. "Possibly nothing, but I found this caught by the wall on the stairs. Rather old-fashioned coat with distinctive buttons. The body—"

Shoving a piece of cake into her mouth, Motts tried to gather her thoughts. She hated thinking about discovering Mrs O'Connell. Her friends, thankfully, kept silent while she chewed.

"I can't quite remember her clothing, but I sent a photo to Teo. I imagine he'll swing around sooner rather than later." Motts hoped the inspector wasn't upset with her find. "My nan has a coat like this."

"Everyone's nan has a version of this coat." Vina leaned in to inspect the button. "There's a weird hole."

Motts shifted forward and noticed the almost pin-sized hole in the fabric. "How strange. Maybe she had a broach?"

Vina spread the fabric out. "Too large."

The inspection and debate over the hole and the button continued through their breakfast. Motts wisely tucked the piece into her pocket for protection. Teo wouldn't be impressed if she handed the evidence over covered in sticky honey and coffee.

She was on her second mug of rich, spiced coffee when Teo messaged her. "Might want to throw one of those English breakfast pasties into the oven. We're about to be invaded by the police."

"We'll make a plate for him. Bless the poor man, having to deal with the three of you." Cadan had joined his wife by the oven. He shook a rolling pin at his twins. "Shouldn't you two be getting the café ready to open?"

With plenty of whinging, the twins left Motts in the kitchen while they got to work. Cadan winked at her before grabbing Leena and dipping her low for a kiss. She watched them make quick work of folding pastries and dropping them onto a tray ready to go in the oven.

When the twins returned to the kitchen, they brought Teo with them. The detective inspector, as per usual, stood taller than everyone. He ducked down to avoid a low hanging light.

"Motts." He sat down across the table from her

when Leena practically shoved him into a chair. The Griffin matriarch feared no one and charmed everyone. When she smiled, Motts could easily see how she'd been a star in Bollywood all those years ago. "Are you trying to become the paper-folding detective?"

"She would fit in with you being the knitting detective." Vina gave him a pointed glare before setting a frothy cappuccino in front of him. "None of your plodding constables found anything by the docks."

"Vina." Motts didn't think the detectives had gotten a chance to explore the harbour. "Don't be prickly. Prickly pear pointedly persists."

"Seven and a half," Vina retorted.

"What? It's a solid ten out of ten on the alliteration scoreboard." Nish grabbed his sister by the arm. "We'll be over here, pretending not to listen to your morning coffee date with your detective."

Teo didn't crack a smile at the antics of the twins. He held his hand out toward Motts. "Show me."

Motts retrieved the fabric out of her pocket and offered it to him. "It might be nothing, but if she wore a coat, you ought to be able to match up the patterns and buttons. There's a strange hole."

"Is there?" He tilted the fabric up to the light.

"Thin. I obviously can't give you any details of the case."

A strangled complaint made Motts peer over to where Nish appeared to be smothering his sister with an apron. Leena was leaning against her husband, laughing herself silly at her children. Teo continued to focus his attention on a small scrap of evidence.

"Teo?" Motts shifted her chair around the table to sit next to him. "Is it hers?"

He eased an evidence bag out of his pocket and carefully sealed away the swatch of fabric. "Have dinner with me? I can bring something over. Say about seven?"

"Date night?" Motts whispered. She glared over her shoulder at her laughing friends. "Okay."

Despite having dated Vina for years and having been casually going out with Teo for a few months, Motts still found it hard to believe. She'd never expected to meet an asexual detective in Cornwall. He was perfect.

And most importantly, Teo never pressed her for more time together. He did a better job than most at knowing Motts required space to herself. She appreciated the gesture immensely.

"We'll talk about this then." Teo pocketed the evidence. "What else have you been up to?"

The conversation shifted to other things as the Griffins joined them for a quick breakfast. With the café needing to be opened, Motts and Teo left the family to their work. She headed out the side exit while he went out the front.

"You found my nan."

Motts had wheeled her bicycle down the alley and paused in front of the café. She looked at the brown-haired, blue-eyed man. "Who's your nan?"

"How many dead old women do you find?" he snapped at her.

Motts kept her bicycle between them. "I had the misfortune of spotting someone in the sea."

"What did you see?"

She didn't like the angry man and was reasonably certain he was the older and taller of the two brothers who'd argued at the church. *What did I see when? How do I answer when I don't understand the question fully?* She was frozen with indecision.

"Jasper O'Connell." Teo strode out of the café towards them, inserting himself between Motts and the man. "You were supposed to meet with Inspector Ash and myself yesterday. Any particular reason you didn't show up? I'd think you'd want answers for what happened to your grandmother."

"I was out fishing."

Motts had learned enough about the local fishing business to spot a lie. "Boats weren't out yesterday. They went early this morning, right before high tide."

"I have my own boat."

"Do you?" Motts stared at Jasper. "What kind of boat?"

"Motts." Teo rested his hand on her shoulder. "Why don't I escort Jasper to his interview? I'll see you later."

"Fine." Motts hoped he'd share at least a few details with her later. "Cactus will be missing me."

Chapter Nine

Her plan for the day had been to finish up a quilling project, but Motts's morning discovery and confrontation with one of the O'Connells had destroyed her concentration. She threw in the towel an hour before lunch.

Quilling and origami required patience and skill. Motts's fingers refused to cooperate. She decided to brave the coastal path.

Since her walk with Dempsey, Motts thought maybe her fears had been settled. She pulled on a light cardigan and headed out her garden gate.

"This is why I moved out here from London." Motts breathed in deeply and enjoyed the salty taste of the sea breeze. "Despite the dead bodies, it's beautiful out here."

The crashing waves on the cliffs below serenaded her along the trail. Motts wondered if her next quilling art should be something related to the ocean. She hadn't created one for herself in a while; one of the downsides of her hobbies being her source of income was she rarely indulged for the fun of it.

"It's you."

"Is it?" Motts came to an abrupt halt on the path. She found herself confronted by the second of the O'Connell brothers. Mikey. "Could you move, please?"

"Someone in the village claimed you discovered Nan's body." Mikey shoved his hands into his pockets. He continued to block her way but didn't stalk towards her as his brother had. "I know it's a cheek, but can you tell me anything?"

"Anything about what?" Motts didn't understand what the O'Connell brothers thought she might know. "I didn't see much. I spotted her floating in the sea. Maybe caught up on some of the rocks. A detective was with me. He might've noticed more than I did."

Unlike his impulsive and aggressive brother, Mikey seemed genuinely moved by his nan's death. Jasper hadn't been grieved so much as enraged about some aspect of the discovery. She wondered why Mikey was up on the coastal path.

"I'm sorry. I don't know if I can be much help to you." Motts considered a hasty retreat since her way forward was blocked. "Do you walk up here often?"

"No. Hate heights. Not overly fond of the sea either."

"Pity, since you live in a fishing village." Motts wondered if he might be lying. She wasn't the best judge of deceit. "Don't you and your brother own a boat?"

"Me? And Jasper? We'd drown each other if we ever went out to sea together." Mikey wrapped his arms around himself. "He doesn't approve of me."

"Oh?"

"Or the way Nan loved me better." He stepped to the side. "Sorry. I shouldn't have been so abrupt. My head's not been straight since they found her. We'd given up hope, or I had. Three years was such a long time. Mum and Jas didn't care much about Nan even when she was alive, aside from the money."

Money.

What money?

Motts rarely succeeded with small talk, but maybe he'd keep going if she didn't try to pepper him with specific questions. "And you did?"

"Nan ran the company with our granddad for years. She had a head for numbers. He dealt with the fishing blocks while she handled everything else." Mikey gestured for her to walk with him back towards the village. "She encouraged me to follow my dreams. Jasper took over the business when Nan got sick. Mum was supposed to be taking care of her."

"But?" Motts prompted when he fell silent.

"Mum and Nan tended to argue. Granddad spoiled mum. His only daughter." Mikey suddenly seemed to remember himself. "Sorry to have interrupted your walk."

Motts could only stare in confusion while he bolted away from her. *Was it something I said? What an odd conversation. All is definitely not right in the O'Connell family. So, did one of them kill their sickly nan?*

Lost in thought, Motts returned to her cottage. She had too much on her mind to continue with a walk. Turning off the alarm and opening the back door, she allowed Cactus to join her in the garden.

The afternoon flew by. Motts lost herself in tending her various herbs and plants. Not a flower in sight, which would prevent her sneezing fits. She watched Cactus chase butterflies.

"Time for tea." Motts carried Cactus into the cottage. He'd spent enough time out in the sun. "Ready for your snack?"

Her tortoiseshell Sphynx cat required frequent healthy snacks to cope with his high metabolism. His peach fuzz suede-like fur didn't allow him to regulate his temperature well. So despite his enjoyment of playing outside, Motts tried not to let him get overheated or too cold during the cooler months.

"Are you wanting your little cardigan?" Motts smiled when Cactus leapt onto the coffee table and sat beside the knitted jumper. "We'll have to thank Teo again for making this for you."

After a soothing cup of tea and biscuits, Motts turned on a YouTube video. She carried a portable speaker outside and continued lazily pottering around in her garden through the late afternoon. It helped her process her thoughts.

While digging around a patch of basil, Motts considered the temperamental O'Connell clan. She wondered about the truth of the relationship between Jasper and Mikey. The latter seemed greatly affected by his nan's death.

Had they simply been facing their grief when they'd argued at the funeral?

It was possible.

"No Cactus helping you weed?"

Motts jumped in surprise and pressed a hand to her chest. She glared at the detective inspector peering over her fence. "Did you want to scare my heart out of my body?"

"My apologies." Teo hefted a shopping tote up for her to see. "I come bearing gifts of food."

"Apology accepted." Motts stood up and shook the dirt off her jeans. "So, how did your conversation with Jasper the Grumpy go?"

"I can't tell you about the case."

She watched him reach over the fence to unhook the latch on the gate and step into the garden. "I happened to stumble on the second of the O'Connell brothers today."

"Did you?"

"I can't talk about personal conversations." Motts made her way into the cottage, leaving Teo to follow her. She ignored his frustrated huff. "What did your bring for supper?"

"Zagrebački Odrezak." He lifted a covered platter and gently placed it on the kitchen counter. "You might call this a schnitzel cordon bleu. Only my mother makes hers with chicken instead of the traditional veal."

"I sense the presence of pastry." Motts leaned

forward to get a closer view of the bag. "And sugar."

"Fine sense of smell." Teo reached in for a second plate. "Cherry strudel. Extra sugar. Extra cherry."

"Dessert first then?" Motts carefully pulled the aluminium foil off the strudel plate. She was greeted by the sight of powdered sugar covering the flakiest of filo that was wrapped around a sweetened cherry and walnut filling. "Oh. Custard."

Teo lifted the little pot and placed it next to the strudel. "Savoury before sweet."

"As you like." Motts handed him a dinner plate and reached for a bowl for herself. "I'm having strudel and custard."

With a wry chuckle, Teo cut himself a large portion of the schnitzel. Motts dished out a decent piece of the cherry pastry and more custard than was probably healthy. She fancied a sweet treat to get her through the evening.

Despite having gone on several dates with Teo, Motts still found them both stressful and awkward. He did his best to put her at ease. She was grateful that he didn't take her reactions personally.

Even Vina, who'd known her for so long, had struggled at times. Motts sat across from him at the table, deftly keeping Cactus away from their food.

Teo waited until halfway through his schnitzel before bringing the conversation around to the O'Connell brothers.

"How about I give you a few details about our talk with Jasper and you tell me about running into Mikey?" Teo saluted her with his glass when she nodded. "You probably won't believe me when I say he didn't have any insights into his grandmother aside from considering her an annoyingly stingy old bat."

"Charming." Motts dragged a cherry through her river of custard. "Mikey didn't offer anything other than more of a mystery."

"We both clearly have issues with open and genuine communication." Teo smiled at her. "I got the idea the elder brother didn't care for his younger sibling."

"And vice versa. I saw them arguing at the church before the funeral. Mikey did mention his mum didn't enjoy caring for her mother. Who inherited the most with her death?" Motts had been wondering about Nadine O'Connell's will. She hadn't been declared dead despite being missing for so many years. "Or, maybe the question is who benefited the most from her death not being discovered?"

"What?"

"They never declared her dead, did they? Mrs O'Connell. If she wasn't dead, who gained controlling interest over the family business?" Motts grabbed a second bowl and dished up some of the cherry dessert for Teo. "And if she hated caring for her mother so much, why not send her to a home for the aged?"

"You keep her at home to control her." Teo tapped his spoon against the bowl. "We've put in a request for a copy of the will. I'd wager the killer discovered the money wouldn't go to them, so if she was missing...."

"It's one theory."

"Murder tends to have only a few motives. Money being one of them." He scooped up a mouthful of pastry, pausing to consider while he chewed. "It's the strongest motive in this case."

"Unless her daughter truly loathed her. I doubt caring for a sickly relative improved an already strained relationship." Motts wondered what Mikey had meant about his mother and brother caring about the money. "How well was their business doing?"

"Another aspect we're investigating." Teo was methodically working his way through the cherry pastry. "Unlike all those true crime shows on the telly, things don't happen overnight with proper police work."

"Proper police work?"

"The kind without flashy detectives and made-up science."

"You're a little flashy." Motts stared into the remnants of her dessert. *A little flashy? I am so hopeless with the flirting and complimenting.* "Forensic accounting takes time."

"Precisely."

Totally.

Completely.

Hopeless.

Chapter Ten

Morning came far too early for Motts. She'd planned to sleep in, but even with the curtains drawn tightly, her plan had failed. Insistent knocking on her front door had her stumbling out of bed in a right state.

"I'm sorry to have woken you up." Detective Inspector Byrne had two cups of coffee in his hand. "One half of the Griffin twins insisted you'd be out in the garden by this time."

"I usually am." Motts shoved her hands into the pockets of her rubber duck pyjama bottoms. "Rough day in the garden yesterday so I slept in."

"Rough day in the garden?"

"My attempts at humour aren't brilliant before coffee." She stepped back to wave him into the cottage. Cactus sidled up to his legs with an inquiring meow. "He hasn't had his breakfast yet. I thought you'd be halfway to London by now."

"A few more questions."

"Oh." Motts dragged her fingers through her hair in an attempt to straighten it from a mop into something resembling a hairstyle. She gave up and grabbed a stray beanie off the back of the couch to drag onto her head. "About Jenny?"

"In a way, yes. How well do you remember the other girls in your class?"

"Not even a little. I think I've blocked out my school years. I couldn't tell you their names. I might recognise them in pictures. Maybe." Motts wandered into the kitchen, stumbling over Cactus, who tried to wind his way between her legs. "Yes, I know, we're late for your breakfast and your walk. Patience is a virtue."

"Don't think felines come with virtue pre-installed into their programming." Dempsey made himself comfortable in one of the kitchen chairs. He set both cups of coffee on the table. "What else can you remember about your classmates?"

Motts rubbed the back of her neck absently. "Hang on."

Leaving the detective inspector in the kitchen,

Motts made her way upstairs into the spare room. She dug around in the closet to find a small wooden chest buried underneath her winter cardigans. *Bingo. There you are.*

Motts carried the little box downstairs and placed it on the table. She opened the lid to pull out a collection of old photographs. "I try to avoid these. Bad memories. I haven't wanted to dig too far into the past despite my periodic searches for information on Jenny's death."

"A birthday party?" Dempsey flicked through the photographs. "Yours?"

"No." Motts shuddered. "One of my classmates. Not Jenny. Mum made me go. She thought I should socialise more."

"How did the socialising work out for you?"

"Dismally. They locked me in a cupboard. Jenny found me. She stole some of the money from the birthday girl's card. We went around the corner for ice cream." Motts had forgotten about their adventure. They'd gotten a comic and a Cornetto each. "My dad found us sitting on a bench in a garden across the street. He bought us a second treat for being clever girls."

"Clearly not the disciplinarian of your family," Dempsey teased.

"No." Motts knew her dad had tried to make up for her mum's constant attempts to "help." "I've genuinely tried to forget most of those horrid girls. We didn't keep in touch. Who does with primary school classmates?"

"You'd be surprised."

She went over to drop two slices of bread in the toaster. "Want a slice?"

"Just the coffee." He lifted his cup in one hand while continuing to peruse her old photos. He flipped one over. "Jenny, Pineapple, Autumn, and Gracie."

Motts placed Cactus's breakfast on the counter for him. She came over to look at the names written by her mum on the photograph. "Autumn and Gracie. They were the least horrid of our classmates. I think their mums knew Jenny's and mine. We were always being thrown together and wandering off on our own when no one was looking."

"Your mum wrote names on all of these. Can I make copies?" Dempsey had pulled out a collection of the photos.

"Keep them. I haven't opened that chest in fifteen years at least." Motts had honestly thought she'd thrown them away. "So clearly I won't miss the photos."

"Thank you." He slipped several of the photos into an envelope she offered to him. "I'll be heading to London today. Time to get back to work."

"Oh?"

"You've answered what you can. No point in my hanging around to enjoy the sea and sun." He saluted her with his cup of coffee. "I'll keep in touch, if you don't mind. I might have more questions for you as my investigation continues. Cold cases are rarely solved without extensive work."

"Friends." Motts kept her focus on her toast, buttering the cooled slices and adding more lemon curd than was probably healthy. "Friends?"

Dempsey broke into a smile when she risked a glance over at him. "Most definitely. I promise to do my absolute best to bring peace to Jenny."

She pressed her knife too hard into her toast, ripping it in half. "You'll bring peace to her family. Not to her. I don't believe the dead are bothered one way or the other. Justice is for those left behind."

"A sober view."

"An honest one. A blunt, practical, and less poetic view." Motts shrugged. She'd had quite a few debates, both friendly and volatile, about her views on death. "Would Jenny want justice? I imagine she would. I'd want it."

"True enough." He continued drinking his coffee and perusing the remaining photos. "My gut feeling is the answer lies somewhere with your classmates or the school."

"Someone targeting our class?"

"Perhaps." Dempsey waved off her second offer of toast. "Not deep enough into the investigation yet. I've requested a number of missing person files along with the school's roster."

"There was a fire." Motts remembered her mother mentioning it. "Would the files have been lost?"

"Still waiting for the school to respond. They don't seem to be in a hurry, which is odd."

Motts munched on her first piece of toast. "Privacy concerns?"

"People don't often ignore a request from the police."

"Don't they?"

Dempsey chuckled into his coffee. "Fair enough. They do. I didn't expect a school to."

"Why not?" Motts had read up on enough crimes to know schools might be even more prone to scandals and secrets. "Can't you force them to respond?"

"Not without something concrete." Dempsey got to his feet. He drained his cup and dropped it into the rubbish bin. "I'll get out of your hair. I want to chat with your detective inspector before I return to London."

"He's not a possession. We're dating." Motts didn't honestly think they'd been together long enough to claim anything other than that. She'd never understood the drive to define relationships instantly. "He is a detective inspector."

"Right." Dempsey chuckled. "I'll chat with the detective inspector with whom you are acquainted."

Once the detective inspector had gone, Motts tried to return to her regular routine. After breakfast, she made quick work of a simple rose origami bouquet. A plaintive meow from Cactus drew her out into the garden to enjoy the late morning sun.

"Well? What are we going to do about our mystery?" Motts stretched out on the grass, enjoying the sounds of the sea drifting over the fence. Cactus leapt up onto her stomach. "I agree. I suppose we're going to need to brainstorm, which means snacks and people."

Though Motts felt more strongly about the snacks than the people, she invited Marnie, River, Nish, and Vina over for an early dinner. They all promised to bring something edible. A potluck of sorts to keep their minds fuelled for the difficult task of solving a mystery.

"My Perry insisted on joining us in a purely unofficial capacity." Marnie dragged her husband into the cottage. "He's promised not to disrupt our dabbling with a criminal investigation."

Motts shifted uneasily. She liked Detective Inspector Ash, but she hadn't expected an uninvited guest. "Okay."

"Hello, Cousin Pineapple." River scooted between Marnie and her husband. He looped an arm around Motts to guide her down the hall into her kitchen. "We tried talking her out of bringing him."

"You bring your boyfriend. Vina brings her girlfriend when she's in town. It's only fair Marnie brings her husband." Motts tried to approach the subject logically. Practically. It's how she dealt with life. "I don't mind."

"You do. He's an unexpected presence in your personal space." River kept his voice low. "I can have a quiet word with him. Perry's a good bloke. He'd leave if I asked him."

"No." Motts grabbed River's arm to hold him by her side. "I won't be rude. He's been perfectly lovely to me."

"Perry's quiet enough. You might never even know he's here." River lifted up the bag in his free hand. "Mum made your favourite."

Opting to ignore the presence of the police officer, Motts helped everyone get food spread across the table. They had a spiced bread pudding from Marnie, the twins had brought a lamb biryani, and River had his mum's dumplings. She added her own dish to the mix—a simple salad along with a drink for everyone to share.

"Dig in." Motts had already put plates and cutlery on the table. She could forget Perry as long as she had food to distract herself. *Well, they can't say I'm eating my feelings. Or, maybe I am.* "We can chat about the case when we finish eating. Or while, if you can keep from being gross."

"Thanks, Motts." River nudged her with his elbow. "You make me feel all warm and fuzzy."

"Weird." She stepped around her cousin and handed out napkins to her guests. "Fever? You're not contagious, are you?"

"No, I'm not." River shook his head with a laugh. "I can't tell if you're genuinely misunderstanding or simply messing with me."

"A novel experience for you. Welcome to my world." She snagged a dumpling from her cousin's plate. "I was joking. I know what warm and fuzzy means."

Only because Uncle Tomato explained it in great detail to me once, but no one else needs to know.

As Motts feared, no one aside from Marnie felt at ease discussing anything related to investigations in front of Perry. Proving his skills at detecting, he made a polite withdrawal after dinner. Motts was ashamed to admit she felt an immense sense of relief at his absence.

And she did.

They grabbed hot chocolates and made their way into the living room to get comfortable. Motts curled up on one of the easy chairs with Cactus at her side. She sipped her drink and allowed the tension to ease away.

"Well?" Vina, ever the patient one, interrupted the momentary quiet. "What have you discovered?"

"Not much." Motts hadn't gathered her thoughts from being thrown off by Perry's surprise presence. "The O'Connell brothers are odd. I imagine Teo won't tell me anything about the button and fabric."

"Did you take a photo?" Marnie asked.

Motts grabbed her phone and quickly found the image to hold out to her. "Do you recognise it?"

"Looks like my Nan's coat." Marnie glanced

around when the others laughed. "I'd swear Nadine O'Connell had one like it, though. Have you spoken with Amy?"

"Amy?" Motts hadn't heard of anyone by the name related to the case.

"Her daughter. The boys' mum. She'd know since she cared for poor Nadine until she went missing," Nish answered. "What if we go casually offer our condolences?"

"Casually?" River chimed in while chuckling into his mug. "Marnie should go. She knows the family."

The rest of the evening was mostly them offering thoughts on the brothers. Motts hadn't learned anything useful. She snuck her phone out to text Nish with a plea for help; she'd reached her limit of social interaction for the day.

Nish checked his phone a few seconds later and made a show of yawning. "Why don't we wrap this up? We're not solving world peace in a night."

River glanced between his boyfriend and his cousin before nodding. "Home it is."

"Let's go, then." Marnie caught her arm, holding her back from following the others to the door. "I'm sorry, love. I should've thought before bringing Perry. He wanted to enjoy an evening together. Next time, I'll ask well in advance to allow you to decide."

Motts shrugged uncomfortably. "It's okay."

"I'm sure it isn't." Marnie smiled, then followed the others down the hall out of the cottage. "Don't forget to lock up behind us."

Chapter Eleven

"Post sensory overload hangover. Brilliant. And all I drank was hot chocolate." Motts woke to an insistent paw poking her eyeball. "Yes, Cactus, I'm aware the sun is up and the alarm is going. If you were extra clever, you could turn it off for me."

Meow.

"My apologies. I'm failing you." She shoved the blanket off her, sat up slowly, and cringed at the dampness around the collar of her T-shirt. "Sodding hot flashes. Useless things."

Meow.

Deciding a shower was a must. Motts hopped under the icy-cold stream and instantly regretted the decision. She dashed out, teeth chattering and cursing every aspect of the morning.

Motts stared down at Cactus, who sat patiently in the bathroom doorway. She grabbed her large and fluffy bathrobe to wrap around herself. "Well, breakfast can only improve the day, right?"

Cactus followed her downstairs, through the small cottage and into the kitchen. Motts put the kettle on, dropped two pieces of bread into the toaster, and then stretched out on the floor to stare up at the ceiling. She contemplated her life choices until the kettle whistled.

Coffee and lemon curd on toast mildly improved her view of the world. Cactus happily munched on his morning snack. Motts clutched her warm mug and tried to pull her thoughts together.

Marnie had promised to pick her up so they could visit with Amy O'Connell. Motts couldn't help wondering what Detective Inspector Ash thought of his wife aiding and abetting an amateur investigation into his case. *Not my marriage, not my confusing conundrum.*

Ten minutes later, Motts rushed around getting dressed, making sure her pets had snacks and water, and locking up. She sat outside on the bench in her front yard, waiting for Marnie. Clouds were gathering in the distance; they were in for a summer storm.

"What on earth did the morning do to you?" Marnie asked when Motts grumpily got into the car. "Maybe we should stop for a cup of tea. It'll sort you right out."

During the summer months, traffic was restricted in the village. Tourists had to park at the top of the hill and walk or take a cab down. Most chose the former; the weather and narrow streets made for picturesque strolls.

"What exactly is the wrong side of the bed? How is there a good or bad? It's just the floor... and the edge of the mattress." Motts considered the phrase all the way through the village. "How is one different from the other?"

"Just a turn of phrase."

"Everyone always says it's 'just a turn of phrase,' but words mean things. You say them for a reason." Motts had, over the years, spent many hours researching where specific idioms came from in the hopes of understanding. "Want to swing by the café for coffee and whatever new invention they have?"

"After." Marnie patted her arm. "We can reward ourselves for being polite."

"Why would we need to reward ourselves?" Motts frowned.

"You've met both Mikey and Jasper, right?" She

continued after Motts nodded, "Jasper gets his charming personality from his mum."

"Brilliant." Motts didn't know if one side of the bed or the other was better or worse. She did know her mood occasionally flared, another wonderful addition to her life since perimenopause showed up. "Will she even chat with us?"

"Amy O'Connell? Resist the urge to gossip about her mum? Doubtful. You'll see." Marnie looped her arm around Motts's, guiding her down one of the narrow lanes, then up a steep set of stairs. The old O'Connell cottage was on the opposite side of the village from hers. "Here we are. Cheerful place."

Motts stared at the cottage. It looked like something straight out of an Edgar Allen Poe poem. She glanced around half expecting a raven to be guarding the place. "Cheerful is certainly a word."

"Don't ring the bell. You'll disturb Bob." A scratchy voice yelled out from the cottage before they'd even come all the way up the walk. "Door's open if you must bother me."

Cheerful soul.

"Bob?" Motts whispered, glancing over at Marnie, who was smothering her laughter into the crook of her elbow. "Who is Bob?"

"Her dog. A small, wiry, bitey version of Amy."

Marnie managed to pull herself together by the time they got to the door. "We're coming in, Amy."

"Well? Come on then. I'm not making tea, so don't ask."

And this is a woman who cared for her ailing mother?

Motts didn't know what to expect when they made their way through the cottage. The hallway with old family photos and shelves filled with immaculate porcelain dolls was beyond creepy. She wanted to run back to the door and far away from the mothball-scented, claustrophobic air. "What on God's green earth?"

"You been hanging around Hughie again?" Marnie teased.

"Quit your muttering and get in here if you must interrupt my morning," Amy shouted once again. Her words punctuated by an angry yapping. *Bob, obviously.* "Well?"

From the voice and the crotchety words, Motts had created a vision of Amy O'Connell in her mind as someone who would fit right into Hansel and Gretel without a problem. In reality, she appeared like a mild-mannered woman. She had pale, watery blue eyes and equally pale skin, with her honey-brown hair pulled so tightly into a bun that not a single hair dared be out of place.

"Hello, Amy." Marnie stood by the sofa across from the armchair where Mrs O'Connell sat with the scruffiest terrier Motts had ever seen. "Should we sit?"

"If you must."

Meticulous.

Despite the massive number of dolls and photos, the entire cottage had an air of almost clinical organisation. It made Motts uncomfortable. *She's certainly something. What must it have been like to grow up in a cottage with all these porcelain faces staring at you?*

Everything was clean. Motts didn't see a speck of dust on a picture frame. The place smelled of the industrial cleaners used at a hospital.

Motts shuddered at the thought. *What do I say? Condolences? That's what people usually say, right?* "I'm sorry for your loss."

"She wasn't a loss." Amy O'Connell's calculating gaze swung in her direction. "You're living in Daisy's cottage."

"My auntie. Yes." Motts blinked at the sharp change of topic. "She left the cottage to me."

"You found a body." Amy patted Bob on the head

when he woofed at the intruders into his space. "Two, given you stumbled on my mother."

"We wanted to offer our condolences," Marnie interjected into the conversation. "I can't imagine having to wonder for three years."

Amy huffed at Marnie. "My mother and I were chalk and cheese. You know this. Why are you here pretending as if you think I'm sobbing my heart out into one of her hideous crocheted pillows?"

The conversation danced around for a few more minutes. Marnie kept trying to coax Amy into casual chat. It wasn't working.

Motts was beginning to reach the limit of her ability to sit in the cottage. The dolls' eyes all seemed to focus on her. "Did you kill her?"

"*Motts*," Marnie hissed.

"What? She doesn't want to natter on about her. She obviously hated her." Motts hadn't seen a point to trying to be subtle any longer. "Someone murdered her mother. And she's not broken up about it."

"Get out, you nosy cows!" Amy cursed them all the way out of the cottage. Bob followed, nipping at their heels. "Why don't you find the poxy scumbag who skulked around the village the summer my sainted mother went missing?"

Motts stared at the door that had been slammed in their faces. She shoved her hands into her cardigan pockets. "Well, she's definitely not going to invite us to tea ever again."

"Was this your idea of good cop, 'slam them in the face' cop?" Marnie asked.

"What?" Motts carefully wound her way down the stairs toward the village. "Time for our reward. We learned two interesting facts."

"Oh?" Marnie caught up to her at the base of the steps.

"Amy O'Connell hated her mother. She kept a meticulously clean house, so being around germs was probably not high on her priority list. Or did she sanitise the cottage from top to bottom after the body was found?" She considered all the family photos she'd seen. "None of those pictures looked like they were of someone Nadine's age. It was all Amy and her horrid son, Jasper. Mikey wasn't anywhere to be seen either."

"The prodigal son verses the favourite?"

"Maybe." Motts dodged an excited family of tourists bustling down the pavement toward the harbour. She winced at the loud shouts from the children. "Coffee? And we mustn't forget the skulking scumbag."

"She means hiker. There were loads that summer. I remember." Marnie followed her toward Griffin Brews.

In the short time they were at the O'Connell cottage, holiday visitors had already begun to arrive. Motts regretted not bringing her earbuds with her. She usually kept a spare pair in her pockets to dull the noise and save herself from a sensory overload meltdown.

"Come on. I'm sure the twins will have a warm cuppa for us." Marnie caught her sleeve and gently led her around another couple, both with cameras around their necks. They made it into the café. "Oh, curry and chocolate croissants. Don't let me eat more than two."

"Hello, dearies." Leena spotted them first. She came over to give Motts a hug. "Hmm, I believe you need some quiet. Into the kitchen with you both."

"I'm fine," Motts tried to insist. Leena knew her well enough to ignore her protests.

She got them settled at the small table in the corner of the kitchen with two mugs of their special blended hot lattes and a few croissants. "Eat up."

Nish joined them halfway through their first croissant. He dropped into one of the chairs, sending up a cloud of flour around him. "How'd your visit go?"

"I asked if she murdered her mother," Motts admitted.

"So, brilliantly then?" Nish stretched an arm behind him to snag a few treats straight out of one of the trays. "Here. These are only just cooled. You'll enjoy these. A baked sweet with a mixture of dark chocolate, coconut, and cashews. We combined our traditional Barfi treat with all the ingredients of a brownie."

Motts inhaled the square treat. "I could scarf down the entire tray."

"Brilliant. Vina will be pleased. She came up with the idea with Amma." Nish grabbed a second one to split and share with her. "Did you learn anything about Amy?"

"Clean. Very clean. Too clean." Motts stared down at the crumbs on the table. She wondered what design it would create to play connect the dots with them. "She definitely hated her mother."

She kept thinking back to the photos on the wall in the O'Connell cottage. And the lack of Nadine or Mikey. What did he think of his mum's behaviour? She made a mental note to try to talk with him again.

What could it hurt?

He might tell me something he wouldn't say to Perry or Teo. They can intimidate without even meaning to do so.

But first, I'm having another not-brownie.

Returning home an hour later, Motts had never appreciated her cosy cottage more. The soft, faded carpets her auntie had bought once upon a time on her travels. The bright paintings, photos, and quilled art on the walls. The soft fleece blankets were strewn across the back of her sofa and armchairs. It felt comfortably lived in.

The O'Connell place had been a strange, creepy mausoleum of a cottage.

Meow.

And her cottage had living creatures, not rows of beautiful porcelain dolls with dead eyes.

Chapter Twelve

"Chocolate?"

Motts briefly regretted not changing out of her incredibly soft turtle pyjamas and bunny slippers before answering the door. She shrugged internally. If Teo had an issue with her clothes, it was his problem, not hers. "Chocolate?"

Teo lifted the small box in his left hand. "I come bearing gifts in the hopes you'll tell me about your visit with Amy O'Connell."

"Good cop?"

"What?" Teo stepped inside when she waved him into the cottage. "Nice slippers."

"Soft." Motts picked up Cactus, who'd come to inspect their visitor. "Had coffee yet?"

"A few." He followed her through the cottage and

watched her open the windows and back door. "Fresh air?"

"Feeling claustrophobic." Motts had suffered nightmares about walls closing in and a porcelain doll. "Mothballs and cleanliness."

"Mothballs and cleanliness?" Teo sat in what was fast becoming his armchair. Cactus leapt up to perch on his thigh. "Did you go visiting Amy O'Connell?"

Motts curled up on the sofa, perusing the selection of Kernow Chocolate bars Teo had brought to her. "Oh. White Chocolate and lemon meringue. My favourite combination."

"Mothballs," Teo prompted when she silently considered her bounty of chocolate.

She refused to fidget under the weighty stare of the detective inspector. "We offered our condolences."

"To a bitter woman who didn't give a damn about her own mum? In my unofficial opinion." Teo reclined into the chair, allowing Cactus to make himself at home in his lap. "Did you pick up anything? She was rather dismissive of my questions. Strange, considering Nadine O'Connell had been missing for three years. You'd think the family would want answers."

"Come sit in the kitchen so I don't have to shout."

Motts hated raising her voice. She'd gone through a dreadful time at school where her teachers alternated between remonstrating her for being too quiet or overly loud. "Want a coffee?"

"I have a feeling I'm going to need one." Teo carried Cactus into the kitchen with him. "Has this one had his walk yet?"

"Not quite." Motts had hit the snooze button on her alarm a number of times this morning. "We had a rough time sleeping. Who inherited the O'Connell business and money?"

"Mikey."

"Mikey?" Motts paused in the process of pulling mugs out of the cupboard. "I thought the elder son, Jasper, ran the business. And wouldn't Amy have inherited directly from her mother?"

"You'd think." Teo absently patted Cactus on the head, earning his eternal adoration. "There wasn't any love lost between them."

"The whole family?" Motts had seen a lot of animosity between the brothers. She couldn't imagine Amy O'Connell being inclined to kindness to anyone, including her own sons. "That cottage could make me want to murder someone."

"It has an aura about it."

"Like a horror movie." She shuddered. "Never

seen a house more perfectly suited for a story of a doll coming to life and seeking revenge."

"You have a vivid imagination." Teo accepted the mug of coffee she offered.

"Too vivid. I carefully curate what I watch to avoid nightmares and bizarre dreams." Motts had given up watching most television and movies. YouTube was far safer to ensure she got some sleep. "Can you imagine growing up there?"

Teo was the one to shudder this time. "I'd prefer to never put that visual in my mind. What happened to not investigating?"

Motts shrugged. "My curiosity has gotten the better of me. Naff thing. I apparently come by it naturally."

She hoped finding dead bodies wouldn't become a habit. The one in the garden had been terrifying enough. She didn't know if her mental health could handle a continuing reoccurrence.

Jenny. The poor girl in the garden. Nadine O'Connell in the sea.

Am I cursed?

Don't be silly.

Finishing up putting her usual breakfast together, Motts settled at the table after putting Cactus's breakfast on the counter for him. She bit into her first slice of toast. Everything seemed better with freshly baked bread; she'd have to thank Nish for dropping it off for her.

"Handy having best mates who run a bakery." Teo took a long sip of coffee. "New brew?"

"Mum sent some down from London. She's got a subscription." Motts shook her head and tried not to roll her eyes. "She's tried about fifty different types. Dad says they've enough coffee to last a millennium. He's exaggerating. I hope. I can never tell."

"I'd imagine he's joking." Teo had another drink. "Good stuff."

"Want a bag?" Motts gestured to the cupboard that hid several her dad had sent to her. "I've more than enough. It's a tad stronger than my usual coffee."

"Keep them. It gives me an excuse to come see you for breakfast." He smiled.

"Why do you need an excuse?" Motts frowned at him. "Neurotypical flirting."

Teo's smile morphed into a chuckle. "Always an unexpected take with you."

Deciding to take it as a compliment, Motts focused on her toast. Dating was strange. She didn't think she'd ever get the hang of it.

Motts finished the last bite of her toast and

washed it down with her milky coffee. "Did the torn bit of coat I found help at all?"

Teo eyed her over his mug for a second. "Too early to tell. We know it's part of her coat. It hasn't led us to the killer. I'm pulling all the CCTV footage available in the hopes of identifying ships going out to sea in the days before you found her."

"Amy O'Connell mentioned a hiker in the area around the time her mum disappeared."

Teo's eyebrows went up in surprise. "Did she? You must've riled her up. She said less than nothing to me. Granted, there are hundreds of hikers in the area during the summer. I'll look into it."

Motts decided not to mention her conversation with Callie, not until she'd spoken with her again. She shifted uncomfortably. "What are you doing this morning? Aside from feeding my chocolate hunger? And drinking my coffee?"

He shook his head and reached across the table to grab her hand. "Sometimes, Pineapple Mottley, I just want to spend time with you."

"Right." She stared at his hand in confusion. "You didn't come to the village *just* for breakfast with me."

"It could be a romantic gesture."

"That's not practical." Motts couldn't stop staring

at the crumbs on her fingertips. "Detective inspectors from Plymouth can't hang around Looe and Polperro indefinitely."

"Excellent point. Maybe I'm conferring with an independent source." Teo leaned back in his chair and laughed again when Cactus leapt up onto his leg. "Someone appreciates my presence."

She fidgeted in the chair, considering the tall, broad-shouldered detective across the table from her. "I appreciate your presence even if I'm dismal at the concept of romance and romantic gestures."

"My baka claims everyone has their own language of romance. I'm going to enjoy learning yours." Teo always spoke of his grandmother in such a reverent tone. "She might come to visit in a few months. I know she'd love to meet you."

Motts found herself nodding. *How do I respond to that? We're only dating. Why aren't there books for how to deal with these things?* "Brilliant."

With what seemed like a knowing smile, Teo changed the conversation. He followed her into the garden, where she set Cactus loose on the butterflies. Motts checked on all her herbs and assortment of other plants, pulling a stray weed.

"Someone's tossed an empty cigarette packet."

Teo was standing on the ocean side of her garden, peering over the fence. "Hang on."

"What's going on?"

Teo returned a few minutes later, wearing a pair of gloves and carefully holding a pack of cigarettes. "Do you have a Ziplock bag or a plastic container?"

With Cactus following on their heels, they returned to the cottage. Motts found a small bag that some of her origami paper had arrived in and offered it to Teo. He immediately dropped the empty packet and a handful of cigarette butts inside.

"We'll get a new camera installed to cover the other side of the fence. Someone was definitely hanging out there." Teo removed his gloves and dropped them into her rubbish bin. "Try your best to stay safe."

"Of course." Motts frowned in confusion as he bent forward to drop a kiss on the top of her head and then walked out with a goodbye called over his shoulder. She picked up Cactus, who'd come over to her. "Is it all men who are confusing? Or just the non-autistic ones? Or is Teo a particularly perplexing human?"

Meow.

"I'm not sure either."

Chapter Thirteen

"I'VE GOT TO GET OUT OF THE COTTAGE," MOTTS muttered to herself. She'd spent an hour after Teo left trying to focus on a quilling project with no success. "Maybe I'll cycle to Fowey again. Callie's shop should be open on a bright sunny day like this."

Deciding not to risk her being out, Motts sent a quick email. Instead of Callie, she received a prompt response from Lilith, her wife, who suggested Motts cycle to Looe instead. Callie was in the middle of a guided kayak tour along the coast and up the river into the village.

Looe meant Auntie Lily and Uncle Tomato. And River. Motts decided she could pass the time at the brewery until Callie was ready. The journey to Looe would be faster than Fowey in any case.

And Auntie Lily always had good food.

"Now, you two behave." Motts made sure Moss and Cactus had everything they needed. "Don't throw any parties or invite strangers inside."

Cactus had already curled up by Moss's terrarium. Motts wondered what the two would gossip about in her absence. She got her bicycle out, checking the chain and tyres. It wouldn't do to get halfway there and have a flat.

Of the multiple routes to Looe, Motts enjoyed the narrow lanes going through Oaklands Park. She usually didn't have to battle with masses of tourists. And it reduced her anxiety to not need to worry about lorries or commercial vans.

With the warmth of the day, Motts left her jumper at home; a long-sleeved T-shirt was good enough. She cycled down the hill, through the village, and up The Coombe. Hughie honked his horn from across the street to get her attention.

"Hello, Constable." She smiled when he came alongside her. "Anything I should know on my journey to Looe?"

"A387's backed up with an accident. They're clearing the wrecked vehicles now." He nodded his head in the general direction. "I'd stick with the Longcombe to cut around the jam and reconnect with it. I imagine traffic will lighten up in time for your ride home, though."

"Okay—" Motts was cut off by a sharp horn.

She glanced over her shoulder to find a red-faced Jasper O'Connell practically punching the horn of his van. He was yelling at them to quit blocking the street. Ignoring him, she said a quick goodbye to Hughie and cycled off, leaving the constable to deal with the angry man.

Taking Hughie's advice, Motts hooked a left off the A397 onto Trelaske Lane, then a few rights onto the National Cycle Route. She definitely wouldn't have to worry about traffic jams on it. Angry drivers stuck on their holidays weren't a pleasant thing to deal with on a bicycle.

The path through Kilminorth Woods was one of her favourites. In the distance, Motts could just hear the West Looe River, mingled with the cheerful chirping of birds. The thick trees had leafed out beautifully this summer.

It smelled lovely. Motts sternly told her nose to cooperate. She didn't want an allergy attack from enjoying the scent of all the wildflowers in the forest.

Her journey to Looe went smoothly. There were

a number of walkers and cyclists on the trail, but they all simply waved a greeting and continued on their way. She greatly appreciated being able to commune with nature without the annoyance of small talk.

Arriving in Looe right before noon, Motts sent a text to Callie, who replied that the kayakers had another hour or more of their guided tour. She decided to have a relaxing lunch. No point in rushing if Callie wouldn't show up until after one.

Despite knowing her auntie would be thrilled to share leftovers, Motts fancied a good sandwich and maybe a scone. She sent River a quick message to see if he wanted to join her. It would be easier to deal with one of the Chen-Mottleys rather than all three of them at the same time.

She loved her family. All of them. Her auntie and uncle were calmer than her parents. Well, mostly her mum. Her dad was possibly the mildest-mannered human being on the planet.

But sometimes, Motts didn't want to answer a million questions about her nerves. *Are you doing okay, love? Need anything? Want some help? You poor dear. Life must be so hard for you.* It never seemed to end despite her insistence on being perfectly fine.

And perfectly capable of dealing with whatever life throws my way.

Motts cycled through the village to Quay Road. She locked her bike up on a railing across from Tasty Corner to wait for her cousin, who came jogging up a few minutes later. "That was quick."

"Yes, hello. Lovely to see you," River teased. "I'll forgive the lack of familial greeting for saving me from leftovers."

"Your mum's leftovers are brilliant."

"Yes, but unlike you, I can't eat the same thing every day for a week." River grinned unrepentantly. "What brings you to Looe? It can't be lunch. You can get sandwiches in Polperro. And it's not me. You see me all the time."

"I need to ask a kayaker about a hiker." Motts crossed the street toward the café. She inhaled the lovely sweet smell of baked goods. "Lunch, first. Questions, after."

Ten minutes later, they were sitting at a little table across the street along the river. They'd managed to grab one with an umbrella to block the sun. Motts scooted the chair up closer and began spreading their bounty out between them.

Steak and kidney pie, chilli with extra chips, a crab salad, brie wedges with redcurrant jelly. Motts's mouth watered at the sight. She stole the chips out from under River's fork.

"Oi." He managed to get a fork into a few of the chips. "Share the wealth, Motts."

They mostly evenly split all of the food. River didn't complain, much, when she finagled well over half of the chips. He stole an extra brie wedge as revenge.

Sipping tea and eating their lunch, Motts filled her cousin in on the mystery hiker. He decided to stick around until Callie showed up. She had a feeling his parents would have words about him skipping out of work at the brewery early.

"Are we halving the pudding as well?" River retrieved lemon drizzle cake, lime and coconut cake, and millionaire shortbread. "We might regret all of this by the time we're done."

"When have we ever regretted dessert?"

"Once."

"Pretty sure we were sworn to silence." Motts shuddered at the memory. Years ago, her dad and uncle had taken the two of them on a camping trip. It had gone badly and not just because they'd fed the kids a dessert with a creamy custard well past its due date. "Never been so sick in my life."

"Why don't we split the shortbread, since we

both love chocolate and caramel? You have the lemon drizzle. And I'll take the coconut and lime." River divvied up the treats. They did sneak tastes of each other's cake. "Remember when my dad used to sneak us extra flakes in our ice creams when your family came to Polperro on holidays?"

Their trip down memory lane was interrupted by a cheerful shout from the river. Motts leaned over the railing to see Callie on her kayak. She told them to meet her a little further down the quay.

By the time they finished up their cake, tossed the refuse into the bin, and walked down the quay, Callie and her group had gotten their kayaks out of the river and on top of her slightly dented dark green Range Rover. Motts and River waited until the others had left. Callie joined them, sucking down water from a bottle like she'd trekked across the Sahara.

Callie finally put her water down and breathed out deeply. "Phew. Hard currents today. Glad to be on land."

"Callie, River. River, Callie." Motts waved between them. She hated making introductions; her mum had made her practice as a child. It still gave her anxiety. "Where's Ashby?"

River snorted loudly, then turned his head away,

coughing repeatedly. "I think I know your wife. It's lovely to finally meet you. My cousin was wondering if you had a way of contacting your friend Ashby. She had a few questions about his time in Looe a few years ago."

"That's what I said," Motts muttered. She elbowed River lightly in the side when he snorted again. "I know you're laughing."

"What? Me?" He grinned.

"So, aside from knowing we're definitely inviting you both to dinner because we're clearly kindred spirits, why do you want to know about Ashby?" Callie followed them down the street back toward the café. Their table was thankfully still open, so they grabbed it. "Let me grab a sarnie, and we can chat."

Despite having already eaten more than was healthy, River apparently felt the need for more chips. Motts stayed at the table. She enjoyed the soft breeze off the river and tuned out the chatter from passing tourists.

She liked Looe, but the larger village was a little much for her, particularly in the summer. Polperro had a charm to it without being overcrowded. She was thankful her auntie Daisy had settled there instead.

Callie returned with her sandwich and a topped-up bottle of water. "So? What's happened?"

Motts gave a brief update on the accusations thrown out by the O'Connell family. She didn't believe Ashby was responsible for the murder. It didn't make sense, but he might've noticed something about the family. "He doesn't even have to come to Polperro if he's still traumatised. I want to know what he remembers about his confrontation with Amy O'Connell."

"Why don't I give him a call and see what he thinks? Yeah? I can call you...." Callie trailed off when Motts shook her head rapidly. "I can text you?"

"Texting. Yes." Motts came to the sudden realisation that she'd exhausted her social energy for one day already. She lightly kicked River's foot, sending him a pleading glance. "Tolerable texting tends to treat."

"Not your best alliteration." River wrapped an arm around her shoulder. "Right. My cousin needs to be off. Why don't you call me when you hear from Ashby? I'll see Mottsy tomorrow anyway."

With a quick goodbye, Motts managed to be off on her bicycle. She owed River massively. Despite the clear blue skies, she couldn't shake the ominous feeling in the pit of her stomach.

Opting for the shortest route home, Motts had never been so relieved to see the last turn down into Polperro. She decided to swing by the Griffin café. Nish or Vina could put together a little packet for her to nosh on later for tea; they'd also be kind enough to not press her for conversation.

The screech of what sounded like a squeaky shopping trolley wheel caused Motts to glance around sharply. She had a split second to register a wheeled cart flying across the road. It shot in front of her tyre, hitting it and causing it to lock up.

Motts careened over the handlebars and hit the road with a mighty thud. Her bicycle rolled down the hill out of control, barely missing a passing cabbie, who slammed on his brakes to miss her as she followed her bike. She crashed into the kerb with a painful crunch. "Bugger."

The cabbie and a bystander quickly bundled her into his vehicle. Motts drifted in and out of awareness. She came round more fully in the clinic as the doctor and nurse checked her for injuries, much to her dismay.

"What did I say about being careful?" Teo stepped into the room despite the doctor and nurse protesting.

Motts ignored Teo and focused on the doctor.

The cabbie had brought her (and her slightly bent bicycle) to the Polperro Health Centre, which was thankfully open. She hadn't fancied a trip back to Looe. "Who called you?"

"Hughie. And Perry, after his wife called him frantic about you getting into an accident." Teo had rushed into the doctor's surgery, worried about her. "What happened?"

"Ask the cart. Or the cabbie."

"You're not making sense." Teo glanced over at the doctor. "Is she concussed?"

"No, I don't believe so." The doctor frowned at the detective inspector. He returned his attention to Motts. "I believe you've escaped serious injury. I imagine you'll be sore for several days. I'd stay off your bicycle."

Given her bicycle tyre was ruined, Motts didn't think she'd be on it for a while. Hughie had been by and promised to take it over to a repair shop. They'd hopefully work their magic.

The doctor stepped out of the room, leaving her with Teo. Motts tried not to fidget. Despite the doctor's assurances, she felt every inch of her impact with the street.

"What happened?"

Motts frowned at Teo's nose. "You asked

already. I was minding my own business, cycling down the street. A little wheeled thing. Flat, no tall handle."

"A platform trolley. It had a collapsible handle."

"Yes, that. It flew across the street, connected with my tyre, and I went head over handlebars." She glanced down at her arms and the rips in her T-shirt sleeves. The doctor had applied ointment to her various scrapes. "I'm going to be so sore tomorrow. All I wanted was a cup of chai and something to take home for tea."

"I'm sure your twins will deliver." Teo helped her to her feet. "Why don't I give you a lift to the cottage? I'm thinking you'll want to stretch out on the sofa. Cactus will take good care of you."

Not for the first time, Motts found herself grateful for Teo's calm and quiet nature. He didn't pepper her with questions. She limped out of the health centre and straight into the passenger seat of his vehicle.

Teo got into his car, turning the engine on and then pausing to check his phone. "Village news travels fast."

"Gossip, not news."

"Either. One of your twins will be at your cottage by the time we get there. Hughie said Marnie flagged him down to tell him." Teo pocketed his phone. "Tiny villages are powerful."

"Gossip is powerful. Did you find the cart and who it belonged to?" Motts had something pulling at her memory. She tried not to think too hard in the hopes she'd remember. Where had she seen a hand trolley before? "Jasper O'Connell had one of those. He was delivering fish to Innis a few days ago. He lost control of it."

"How does someone accidentally lose control of a trolley twice?"

"They don't." Motts shrugged, instantly regretting the movement. "Home."

"Home it is." Teo thankfully didn't press for further conversation.

By the time they arrived, Teo had been proven right. And wrong. It wasn't one of her twins. Both Nish and Vina were there.

"Oh, bugger." Motts stared out of the car window at the multiple people waiting in front of her cottage. "I'll stay in here. Thanks."

"Cactus might miss you." Teo reached over to squeeze her hand. "They're only worried. It's never a bad thing for people to care about you being hurt."

Motts sighed.

"They know you're here. They can see you."

Motts sighed. Again.

"I can make them go away for now," Teo offered. "I imagine they'll be back to check on you by the evening."

Deciding not to fight the inevitable, Motts forced herself to get out of the vehicle. Everything hurt. She wanted a hot bath, a YouTube marathon, and space to process the day.

"Mottsy." Vina rushed over. She took Motts's bag and gently led her toward the cottage. "River used his emergency key."

"Of course he did."

River held his hands up in surrender. "Mum made me."

Motts was guided into her own cottage by her ridiculous friends and family. Cactus stayed over by the terrarium, obviously confused by the mild-mannered chaos. Motts shook off Vina's hand. "I can walk fine. I've got bruises and scrapes, not a broken limb."

"You will sit." Her auntie pointed regally toward the sofa. She took control of the room, ordering the twins and River to make tea and plate up the food they'd brought. Her attention turned to the detective inspector, who stood over a foot taller than her. "You. You should hold her hand."

Motts hadn't thought her day could get any more embarrassing than tumbling over her handlebars. She had been wrong. Her aunt ordering Teo around was both horrifying and entertaining. "Auntie Lily."

"Do you not like holding hands?" she asked with what sounded like genuine confusion.

Motts sank into the sofa cushions and dragged a blanket over her head. She pulled it off after a moment. "Auntie Lily."

River deftly darted into the room to drag his mum into the kitchen. His loud whisper carried through the room. "What have I said about asking Motts about her relationship?"

She reached up to pat her son on the cheek. "You're a good boy, caring about your cousin. Such a sweet boy. We raised you well."

Motts muffled her laugh into the blanket. *At least I'm not the only one suffering embarrassment at the hands of Auntie Lily.* She risked a sideways glance at Teo, who'd taken a seat beside her. "I don't *mind* holding hands."

"Neither do I. Fairly confident we've done so a few times already." He watched her family boisterously organise themselves in the kitchen. "Are they helping or hindering?"

"Both." Motts had no doubts Vina and Nish

could talk circles around anyone, drawing out the making of tea to give her time to settle herself. "I'm lucky to have good friends."

"And me."

She leaned into the immense strength of the man beside her. "And you."

Chapter Fourteen

The following morning, Motts woke up not quite feeling like death warmed over but close enough. She was considerably less charitable toward the owner of the wheeled cart. Accident or not, they'd definitely done some damage.

Motts got out of bed slowly and cautiously stretched her body. After kicking everyone out of her cottage, she'd sunk into a warm bath, hoping to stave off some of the soreness. It helped a little.

"If I find the berk who lost control of his trolley, we're having words. Might just be a single word, but it'll be an unpleasant one."

Meow.

"Be kind, Cactus. I'm not myself this morning." She found walking fine, though her scrapes and bruises complained if she went too quickly or reached her arms over her head. "Don't slip between my legs. If I tumble over, I might not get up again. And then where will you be?"

Forgoing her usual toast and coffee, Motts made a hot chocolate spiked with espresso and snagged two of the chocolate curry croissants the twins had brought with them. Yesterday had been difficult. A treat or three was in order.

After setting out breakfast for both of her pets, Motts went outside to sit in the garden with her hot chocolate. Vina had brought her a cushioned lounge chair. She stretched out and tried not to breathe in too deeply, since it made her side ache.

If the cause of her accident had been Jasper O'Connell, how did someone lose control of their trolley twice in the scope of a week? *I'm not even that clumsy.*

Well, I am, but I don't own a hand cart.

Motts had been so wrapped up in her accident, she'd forgotten about her conversation with Callie, who'd promised to reach out to Ashby. "I should've brought my phone outside with me."

Sipping her hot chocolate, Motts wondered if Cactus could grab her phone, open the door, and come outside with it. Probably not. She finished her drink, listening to the happy birds and the ocean in the distance. *I should get my mobile before someone texts and assumes the worst when I don't answer immediately.*

There were, in fact, four text messages from various people and seven missed calls from her mum. Motts listened to the voicemails, each one left with increasing levels of panic. She decided to call her dad in the hopes his calmness would prevail.

"Are you feeling okay, darling? Your mum worries."

"Mum panics." Motts distracted Cactus with a stray crumpled piece of paper. "A lot. Constantly."

"She's your mother. She cares. And caring, for her, involves panicking followed by potentially over-reacting." Her dad's voice had a weird lilt to it.

"No."

"Now, we haven't seen you in months. We'll only stay for a few days," he promised.

He was definitely lying. Motts had no doubts her parents would find a reason to stay for a week or more. She couldn't blame them, given the drive required to get to Polperro from London.

"Where are you staying?" Motts asked the question that she greatly feared the answer to. She didn't enjoy being under the same roof as her mum for any length of time. "Here?"

"Now who's the one panicking?" he teased with a quiet chuckle. "Your uncle Tom tells me the cottage adjacent to them is available for a few days. We'll be in Looe. Does that reduce your stress levels?"

"Dad."

"Darling. You may be a mystery to me at times, but you and your mother never deal well together when she's concerned about your life choices."

Translation: you and your mum drifted apart when you became an adult and in control.

Motts heard footsteps on the other end of the phone and a door closing. "Is it serious enough for you to hide in your office?"

"Listen, darling. Your mum always wanted you to stay in London with us. She'd have stretched to a townhouse nearby. Prepare yourself for an 'I'm only concerned for your safety' type of lecture. She means well. Must go. Love you loads." He disconnected the call before Motts could even say goodbye.

Motts glared at her mobile with a sense of dread. *What now?* She decided to call in reinforcements by texting her cousin and Vina; either would inform Nish as well. *Meow.* "Yes, Cactus. I'm aware you've been stuck inside for far too long. How about we stroll through the garden? I saw at least one stray butterfly waiting for you to stalk."

Her plans were derailed when her doorbell rang. Motts glanced at her phone. No new messages. She doubted her friends would simply show up; they knew better.

She opened the door to find Mikey O'Connell. "Hello?"

"My brother wants to apologise for the accident yesterday."

"I'm sorry. What?" Motts was bewildered by the flowers thrust at her. "Hyacinths?"

"They mean sorry. My nan was obsessed with the Victorian language of flowers." Mikey shifted uncomfortably in front of her. "Your cat doesn't have fur. Is she okay?"

"He's fine. He has peach fuzz. Don't touch him." Motts used her leg to ease Cactus back into the cottage. "Why are you giving me flowers?"

"Jasper."

She tried to keep the hyacinths away from her nose to avoid an allergy attack. "Do you buy flowers for your brother often?"

I am not equipped for this conversation.

"Were you badly hurt?"

"I'll live." Motts kept her free hand on the doorknob. "What was he doing anyway? I don't understand why the cart didn't go downhill instead of toward me?"

Mikey shrugged. "Not a clue. Sorry again."

Motts watched him jog away from her toward the stairs leading toward the village. She put the flowers by the door for Vina to take to Leena. "Apology not accepted."

Maybe Mum will like the flowers.

Leaving them outside the house for the moment, Motts went back inside. She could already feel a tickle in her nose. *I will not give in to the sneezing. I won't.*

On the way into the kitchen, Motts answered a text from her cousin. River intended to drive over to her cottage after swinging by Griffin Brews. He wanted to know if she wanted anything.

She said no.

Meow.

"Yes, Cactus. Your uncle River will probably bring both of us something. He gets it from his mum." She allowed him a tiny extra treat. "I suppose I better change out of pyjamas. He'll tease me about lounging about all day if I don't."

A quick wash made Motts feel slightly more capable of dealing with the day. She winced as moving too much tugged at the scrapes on her arms and legs. River would have to deal with her in a T-shirt and pyjama bottoms; all her other trousers rubbed against her injuries.

"Well, at least these *look* like regular striped trousers." Motts returned to the kitchen to put the kettle on. She wanted another cup of tea to deal with the impending influx of sound. Cactus leapt onto the counter, meowing plaintively. "You've already eaten. I know you're not starved. Plus, Uncle River will bring you a snack."

Meow.

"I know, I'm a failure." She bent down to rub her nose against his fuzzy head. "I'm sure you'll forgive me."

River arrived midway through the mug of tea. He let himself into the cottage after knocking three times. "Leena insisted on feeding you."

"Mums."

"Mums. No matter where they come from, they all think you never eat unless they've fed you." River hefted up the paper bag. "Why are there hyacinths outside your door? Who sent you flowers when you're so allergic to them?"

"Apology."

"Pardon?"

Motts snickered. His response had struck her as fun. "One O'Connell sibling apologising for the other."

"*Pardon?*"

While Motts chatted about Mikey's visit, they perused the wealth of treats from Griffin Brews. River was as confused as Motts. He couldn't explain the strange visit.

"You've failed as my non-autistic translator," Motts joked. River was one of the people she turned to when confused by neurotypical behaviour. "Oh, croissants."

"Leena knows your weakness." River grabbed one of the sweet and spicy pastries for himself. "What shops are near where you fell?"

"I don't remember. What's up at the top of the hill?"

"Why don't we take a walk over to see if any of them have CCTV cameras?" River broke a second croissant in half and offered her part. "Maybe we can see what happened."

"I went over my handlebars."

"Yes, Motts, but were you helped over accidentally or on purpose?" River munched his last bite slowly. "Mikey claimed his brother didn't launch his projectile at you on purpose. Why don't we find out for sure?"

"Purposeful projectile plunged precariously."

"Nice." River raised nine of his fingers up. "Decent score."

Motts snickered into her cup of tea. "Going out means actual trousers."

"Why? Who cares if you're wearing pyjamas? You were injured. Sod anyone who's bothered." River carefully folded the bag down. He set it up into the cupboard. "Can Cactus open doors?"

"Not yet." Motts fed her cat part of the fishy treat Leena had included for him. "He'll be fine. Not sure I want to walk down all those stairs and up the hill."

"We'll drive to the parking up at the top, then walk across the street." River patted her shoulder gently. "Want me to carry you?"

"Don't be a prat."

"Who, me?" He snuck Cactus a tiny flake of croissant. Cactus sniffed it before slinking away to join Moss at the window facing the back garden. "Finicky creature."

"He has taste. You licked your fingers. Germs, River, germs."

"Honestly." River rolled his eyes at her. "He licks—"

"Don't be rude," she interrupted. "I'll risk jeans if we're going into the shops. I won't be a moment. Rude River runs roughly."

"You make it sound as if I've got—"

"Don't be gross. I've just eaten a croissant." Motts cut him off before heading up the stairs to her bedroom.

When Motts returned from swapping soft pyjamas for less soft jeans, River had managed to eat another croissant. He grinned innocently, swiping crumbs from his shirt. She sighed; some things never changed no matter how old they were.

"Well? Ready?"

"Let me set the alarm." Motts remembered the cigarette butts on the other side of her fence. If the accident hadn't been intentional, she wasn't taking any chances. "Want to drive to Fowey afterwards? Callie texted me earlier with news about Ashby."

"And you want to be away from Polperro if your parents decide to arrive sooner than actually possible?" River followed her out of the cottage. He waited for her to lock up. "You know even your mum can't make the drive take less time."

"Don't underestimate her." Motts wouldn't put it past her mum to hijack a helicopter for the journey. "At least they won't be staying in Polperro."

"Small mercies." River checked her over carefully. "Are you sure you're up for this? We can wait until tomorrow."

"My scrapes and bruises will be as sore tomorrow as they are today. I'm okay. No permanent damage done. It only twinges a little."

"A little in Motts speak usually means a lot." River held the door out for her. "You can ask for help."

"I managed to open multiple doors. Fairly certain a car isn't any more difficult." She climbed inside and set her bag between her feet. "I'm fine. Mostly."

"It's the mostly I worry about." River slowly reversed down the hill until he could deftly turn the car around. "Why don't you text Callie to see when a good time to stop by is?"

They parked across from where Motts had crashed her bike and walked over. She stopped at the top of the street, staring down. Her mind replayed the accident repeatedly.

"Struck out at the pub." River joined her. He'd jogged over to talk to the owner. "Their camera is on the fritz. Spoke to Jess at the bookshop. He's going to email me the video from yesterday, just from the accident, maybe a few minutes before. I want to figure out if Jasper saw you before his cart went flying out of control."

"There are cameras in the car park."

"I'd wager either Teo or Perry used their detective inspectorness to get that."

"Detective inspectorness?" Motts smiled at him. "Are we making up words again?"

Since none of the other shops had cameras, they decided to make their way to Fowey. Inspector Ash probably wouldn't let them see the village CCTV footage no matter how nicely they asked. Motts didn't fancy trying her luck.

"We've got time. Fancy a stroll around Polridmouth Cove?"

Chapter Fifteen

"Did you ever wish your parents moved up to London with mine?" Motts followed River down one of the footpaths to one of the two beaches that made up Polridmouth Cove. They strolled along the sand, peering into some of the rock pools exposed by the low tide. "You could've grown up in the city."

"And miss this?" River gestured toward the vast expanse of the sea. "We visited London often enough. I've never wished we grew up there. I did once ask Father Christmas to have you move to Cornwall."

"Did you?" Motts smiled sunnily. She shifted further down the beach, away from a rather boisterous family who were the only other visitors to the cove. "I'm sad he didn't grant your wish. I love it here. So much calmer than London."

River glanced over at the family after a particularly piercing shriek. "Quiet as well."

She kicked sand at him. "You know what I meant."

"I do." River dipped his toes into the rock pool. "Are you really feeling okay?"

"Sore as can be. I won't say I don't hurt. It's not as bad as when I went off my Vespa." Motts bent down to pick up a particularly pretty shell. "Remember when your dad convinced me tiny invisible crabs lived in shells?"

"I remember getting shouted at for stomping on a shell and sending you into a panic." River tucked his hands into his pockets. "Wind's turning chilly."

"It is. We should head back before we catch a cold. Last thing I need in the middle of summer." Motts still remembered her uncle Tom and her cousin both getting into trouble for traumatising her. It was her granddad who explained invisible crabs weren't a thing. "I should've worn a jumper."

"You'd be boiling by lunch if you had." River splashed in the water briefly, then followed her back up the sand. "Come on then. My mum'll force-feed us soup if we so much as sniffle."

On the way to the car, River received a message with the video from Jess. Motts squeezed up next to her cousin and peered down at his phone. He tried to zoom in close enough for a good view of the footage.

"There. Jasper." River poked a finger at the screen. "He's on the corner by the pub with his empty cart. Must've already made his delivery."

"And there I am coming into the frame. Stopping at the light up the street." Motts wished they had a longer view up the hill. She wanted a better perspective on what Jasper would've seen. "He's definitely looking in my direction. Maybe. I don't think we'll ever prove if he was or not."

River kept watching the video. "We can prove it wasn't an accident."

On the screen, the slightly blurry Jasper lowered the handle on the cart then launched it across the street with a solid kick. Motts made him replay the video several times. He also made sure to send a copy to Hughie, just in case the Polperro police hadn't seen it.

They had. Hughie immediately texted to tell them Inspector Ash suggested they leave the detecting to the detectives. Hughie added a few crying laughing emojis to show what he thought the odds of them listening to be.

"Such faith in his fellow human beings." River pocketed his phone. "Right. Well."

Motts leaned against the seat. She regretted getting out of her comfortable, warm bed. Her body was starting to ache again from landing on the pavement and rolling across it at speed. "Callie."

River glanced over at her. "Why don't you stay in the car when we get there? I can have a chat with Callie about Ashby and take notes for you."

"River."

"You look done in. I should've made you stay at home."

"Made me?" Motts had inherited her stubborn streak from her auntie Daisy. "Made. Me."

"Repeating yourself doesn't change the facts. Are you honestly going to tell me you don't wish you'd stayed in bed?" River wasn't going to believe her no matter what Motts said, so she took the easiest course of action and said nothing. "Why don't we ask Callie and her lovely wife to meet us at the little park along Esplanade? It's got those little round picnic tables. We can grab a snack and a cup of tea, then chat. You can stare at the sea if you don't want to take part in the conversation."

Motts couldn't argue with the lunch. "Fish finger butties."

"Oh, good idea. Fish finger sandwiches with a healthy dose of sautéd potatoes. We can split their cheese plate as well. Lifebuoy Café should be open by the time we get there. It's not too far. If we find a decent parking spot, you can grab a table while I take a jog down the street. Or text Callie to grab it for us on her way up." River tapped his fingers against the steering wheel. "Here. I'll send her a message."

Settling into the seat, Motts lowered the window to enjoy the breeze. From a distance, the sound of children playing on the beach wasn't nearly as piercing. She dozed in the comfort of the car while River texted back and forth with Callie.

"Don't forget their peanut butter Oreo fudge." Motts roused herself enough for chocolate. "Think they'd give us a thermos of tea?"

"No, but the hotel across the street might. They've got a restaurant." River slipped his phone into his pocket. He motioned for Motts to get out of the car. They walked the short distance to the park. "Callie will be here with Ashby in about twenty minutes. Her wife's keeping an eye on the shop."

"Tea."

"I'm going to sort out the tea and maybe some

water. You keep our spot." River jogged out of the little park area and across the street toward the hotel.

The picnic benches wound up being slightly uncomfortable for one specific scrape on the back of her leg. Motts stretched out on the grass instead. River didn't bat an eyelid when he found her staring up at the clouds ten minutes later.

He set a basket down on the table and plopped down on the grass next to her. "We showed up before the lunch crowd. They made a nice little picnic basket for us with cups, tea, water, and mini bottles of wine. Quite fancy. The lovely gentleman at the hotel asked us to return the basket, though. So we'll have to be careful. Are we eating on the ground?"

"Soft."

"There's probably a blanket in the boot of my car. We could spread it out at the far end of the park. Give us a better view of the water and more privacy from the street." River hopped up, patted her on the shoulder, and jogged away. "Don't go anywhere."

"Where am I going to go?" Motts asked a stray cloud. It didn't answer. "I was promised chocolate and fish finger butties."

"Are you talking to yourself again?" River reappeared with a blanket over one arm. He grabbed the basket and nudged her very gently with his foot. "Up you get. Help me spread this blanket out."

"Why do you have a blanket in your car?"

"Don't laugh."

Motts glanced sharply over at him. "Why would I laugh?"

"You wouldn't. Most people would." River held a hand up to stop her from responding. "Nish and I enjoy going out to the beach for supper dates."

"Do you?"

"I promise the blanket is clean."

"Did you dust off the sand?" Motts asked. She grabbed two corners and helped him spread it out. She had to wait while he laughed uproariously. "What's so funny?"

River ran his fingers through his hair. "Nothing at all."

"It's a sex thing, isn't it?" Motts made herself comfortable on the blanket. She grabbed the thermos of tea and one of the cups. "I need to fortify myself for the explanation."

River was saved from responding by the arrival of Callie and a scruffy ginger who appeared as though he'd walked off a hiking trail out in the wilds. "Hello, Ash."

"River."

"You know each other?" Motts glanced in surprise at her cousin.

"I didn't realise Callie's Ashby was my old schoolmate Ash." River dragged him into a hug, then introduced him to Motts, who waved. She had no intentions of hugging a stranger. She barely allowed her family to do it. "Pineapple Mottley. We call her Motts."

"Pineapple?" Ashby glance from River to Motts. "Better than being named after some posh twit who'd never give you the time of day."

River shoved Ashby with a laugh. "Don't mind him. He's got issues with coming from an upper-middle-class home."

"Think they have issues with me." Ashby gestured to his slightly messy hair tied back, his scruffy facial hair, and his wrinkled T-shirt and jeans. "My parents don't understand my choice to live out of a caravan and hike through the wilds."

"My mum hates my cottage."

"Motts." River sighed. "She doesn't hate your cottage. She worries. She loves you so much, I doubt anything would be enough for you."

She waved off her cousin, not wanting to get into the conversation. "I know."

"So, I heard you wanted to know about my run-ins with the O'Connells a few years ago." Ashby sat on the edge of the blanket opposite Motts, Callie joined him. They spread out the food they'd picked up. "Felt sorry for the old woman. Nadine? I think she said. I tried helping. She was walking down the lane by her cottage."

"Was she?" Motts had heard from Marnie about Nadine O'Connell being bedridden. "How did she seem?"

"Confused. Kept talking about dolls." Ashby grabbed one of the bottles of water. "Her daughter caught up and began screeching at me. Accused me of kidnapping. All sorts of things. Someone called the local copper. Hughie? Think that was his name. He sorted us out, sent me on my way. Never saw her again. I did have to read the riot act to one of her sons. Red-faced bloke, came up screaming at me. Think he gets that from his mum. I decided to avoid the village. Something wrong with the O'Connell family. Very wrong."

The rest of the picnic went well. Motts ate her sandwich and chocolate, mostly in silence. Ashby had answered her questions about his time in Polperro but left her with loads more about the O'Connells.

River had gotten quite wrapped up in his little reunion. The afternoon wore on, and more people crowded into the park. Motts knew she was reaching her limit of dealing with sound.

"River. *River.*" Motts had to repeat herself a number of times to draw her cousin out of his conversation with Ashby. "River."

"What?" He turned toward her. "Ah. Bugger. Time to go, then."

Some of the building stress must have shown on her face. River had her bundled into the car in impressive time. He said their goodbyes, raced the basket back to the hotel, and got them on the road to home.

And then they got stuck in traffic.

"Sorry, Motts. I should've paid better attention." River switched radio stations until he found the Escape to Cornwall Pirate FM station, which played the sounds of the area. "Here. A little crashing of ocean waves will do you some good."

The short trip from Fowey to Polperro took them what seemed like a century. Motts arrived home, kicked off her trainers, and fell flat onto the sofa. Cactus climbed up to join her.

"You. Me. Moss. And a quiet cottage." Motts shifted to allow him to sit on her stomach. "Your uncle River inherited the chatty gene from the Mott-leys. The one I missed."

Meow.

"Yes, I have forgotten something, haven't I?" Motts shot up on the sofa, groaning when her sore body complained. "Oh, no. Mum and Dad are coming today."

Meow.

"We need reinforcements." Motts dug into her pocket to find her phone. She genuinely didn't want to deal with people at all. Her mum, however, was not one to be deterred. "Let's sort your dinner first."

While Motts got both of her pets fed, she texted with her various friends. Nish and River had plans to drive to Plymouth for a date night. Vina had left to pick up her girlfriend, who'd flown in for another business trip.

Meow.

"You're right. I should text Teo. He did promise to come and sort out the new camera in the garden." Motts rubbed Cactus's head, smiling when he gave her finger a rough lick. "You are a clever boy."

Will Mum and Dad want something to eat?
Probably.

Her refrigerator was filled with leftovers. Motts could already hear her mum complaining about her dietary choices and how her teeth would fall out. *You'd think I was still a spotty teenager, not a grown woman.*

"Well, Teo will be here soon. I have no doubts Mum and Dad will arrive before sunset." Motts knew her parents well. They'd definitely visit her first, then drive over to Looe to where they'd be staying. "Better clean up some. Mum will wander around with a white glove on her hand, looking for dust."

Only a slight exaggeration.

Teo arrived thirty minutes later; her parents showed up like a whirlwind not long after. He'd gone into the garden to sort the new camera. Her dad gave her a hug, then went outside to join him.

Motts stared out the window. "Maybe—"

"Your father is perfectly fine with your young man." Her mum dragged her attention away. "Sit down. Your auntie Lily had some hideous story to tell me about you investigating another crime. Didn't you learn from your last near-death experience?"

"Mum." She picked up Cactus and cuddled him to her chest. He offered a warm, purring comfort in the storm of her mother's disapproval. "I didn't *plan* to find a body in my garden. And I didn't intend to discover one in the sea either."

"You did decide to determine who the killer was." Her mum sniffed delicately.

Stuck inside with her mum, Motts was slowly losing her mind. Her mum had started on the new layout of the living room furniture. It hadn't taken her long to move on to the dangers of Cornwall and how she should move back home to London.

Never in a million years will I give up the quiet of my cottage on the hill.

"Are you listening, darling?"

"I'll fix tea." Motts fled toward the kitchen with a quietly purring Cactus. "Biscuits?"

"Not before supper. You'll spoil your appetite."

"Fine." Motts grabbed the packet of homemade lemon biscuits Leena had made for her and crammed two in her mouth. If she was eating, she would resist the urge to reply.

One of these days, Mum will let go of whatever vision she has in her mind of the perfect daughter. She'll get to know me as an adult. I just hope it happens sooner rather than later. I'm almost forty. I won't hold my breath.

"How goes the tea, darling?" Her mum joined her in the kitchen. She opened one of the cabinets. "Why are your crisps in this cupboard?"

Motts filled the kettle in silence. She grabbed the largest of what had been her auntie's teapots to drop tea into. "My kitchen. My crisps. My organisation methods."

"Wouldn't they—"

"No." Motts narrowly avoided slamming the electric kettle on the counter. Her mum always managed to get a rise out of her without even trying. "I want them over there. What does it matter where the crisps go? I eat them. I buy more. They don't care where they sleep when I'm not munching on them."

Do crisps ever care where they go?

I'm not caffeinated enough to deal with the existential crisis of a thin, crunchy potato slice.

Her mum continued to inspect her kitchen. Motts retreated into herself, falling into a stony silence. She made the tea on autopilot.

Silence had been a refuge as a teenager. Motts found her mum to be an overwhelming force of nature. She'd often sunk into her own mind, losing her ability to put sentences together.

"Are you listening, darling?"

No?

Motts was saved from responding by the return of her dad and Teo. The former went over to her mum while the latter joined her at the counter. "Hello."

Teo rested a steady hand on her shoulder. "Want some help?"

"It's just tea." Motts gripped the counter to keep from giving in to the urge to fling the teakettle. Sometimes, meltdowns needed an outlet. She'd found breaking glass to be quite satisfying but expensive. "I'm fine."

"You use fine far too often." He glanced over at her parents, who were not doing a brilliant job of spying on them. "Perhaps I can encourage them to head to your auntie and uncle's early?"

"Never happen." She felt the room closing in on her again. "I'll be outside. Need air."

Fleeing outside, Motts sat in one of the loungers, allowing the ambient Cornish seaside sounds to calm her nerves. The sun had almost fully set. She heard the door open and close a few minutes later.

"Hello, love. Are you being a good cat?" Motts felt another knot in her release when Cactus leapt up into her lap. She turned slightly toward the cottage to find Teo with a laptop in one hand. "My parents?"

"They received a sudden invitation to your uncle's. They didn't refuse." Teo's smile made him seem quite fierce. "Don't mind me. I want to make sure your system is set up correctly."

She rubbed Cactus's head gently. "Mum loves me."

"I'm sure she does." Teo focused on his computer, occasionally tapping the keys. "There. The new camera is added into the system and working perfectly."

"Thank you." Motts watched the last rays of the sun disappear.

"Why don't I leave? Give you some time to decompress by yourself?"

She reached out to grab his hand. "Stay."

I could use a distraction and a buffer zone if they decide to come back.

Chapter Sixteen

"Hello, darling." Vina mimicked Motts's mum so well, she almost spun around to find a car to hide behind. "Sorry, Mottsy. Didn't mean to scare you."

"Not amusing. And you definitely meant it." Motts glanced around to make sure her mum hadn't followed her into the village. "She came over to the cottage this morning without Dad."

"Oh, no." Vina handed over her cup of coffee. "Here. Have mine. You need the boost. It's a new recipe—chocolate and cherry cold brew; we're still experimenting with the flavours. We can walk and talk. Are you up for visiting the O'Connell business? We can wait until tomorrow."

After Teo had left the night before, Motts had thought over the last few days and the mysterious reappearance of Nadine O'Connell's body. She'd decided to pay a visit to O'Connell Cold Storage; Vina had volunteered to go with her. Her mum showing up before breakfast had definitely been a fly in the ointment.

Walking down by the harbour, they headed up the street toward the O'Connells' business. The façade remained from the original building. Motts imagined the inside had been changed to more modern freezers.

She hoped.

"Bit of a crowd," Vina commented. She gestured to one of the three vehicles parked outside the old building. "Mikey's here. Pretty sure Amy drives the purple Mini."

"What are we going to say about why we're here?" Motts hadn't considered the excuse for snooping around the building.

"We'll tell them Griffin Brews is looking into renting space."

"In a cold storage?" Motts didn't think it sounded terribly believable.

"Do you have a better idea?" Vina tilted her sunglasses down to stare over them at Motts. "No? We'll go with my lie and see what happens. What's the worst thing they can do?"

"Murder their nan?" Motts reminded her.

"Fair point. We'll stick together." She looped her arm through Motts's. "Don't worry. They can't *all* be involved."

"They could."

"Why don't I distract the brothers? You sneak around." Vina leaned in to whisper to her.

What happened to sticking together?

Motts found herself shoved into the warehouse while Vina headed in the opposite direction. "Be careful."

Hearing what sounded like both brothers arguing with their mother, Motts skirted the office. She eyed the rows of matte grey doors. How long did she have before someone noticed her? The warehouse had to be littered with CCTV cameras.

A quick peek into the first walk-in freezer chilled Motts to the bone. She regretted not bringing a jumper with her. After walking through all of them, she'd likely be frozen herself.

Despite the freezer obviously having sufficient space to hide a body, Motts knew local fishermen were in and out of the warehouse. They'd have noticed a corpse amongst the carp.

So, if one of the O'Connells had kept their

murdered nan on-site, where had it been? Not in the walk-in freezers. Maybe one of the chest units?

She'd noticed several chest freezers lined up along the far wall. Two had padlocks on them. Those definitely had the capability of storing a body. Teo had surely inspected those, though.

Wouldn't he?

Do the police need a warrant to search for where a body's been stored? Probably. I should ask Hughie; he won't get all indignant about my poking my nose into the investigation.

Motts snuck over to the row of chest freezers. She tugged lightly at one of the padlocks. *Maybe I should text Teo to ask if he saw these.*

One last walk-in freezer remained. Motts cautiously opened the heavy grey door. She noticed a sign taped to it, warning of a faulty safety release and to use caution entering.

Motts poked her head in, and a hard punch to her back sent her sprawling inside. "What the devil?"

The door slammed shut with a dull thud. Motts blinked in the sudden icy darkness. She used her phone as a torch to find a light switch unsuccessfully.

Moving over to the door, Motts tried to find the

safety release on the off chance the notice had been wrong. It wasn't. No amount of shoving budged the solid metal even a little.

What now?

Nish had once told her about the dangers of walk-in freezers. He'd gone through a safety course on the subject when Griffin Brews had one installed. Motts regretted not paying more attention.

Right.

The vital thing to do is breathe calmly. Is this airtight? Will I suffocate before I freeze to death?

Bad brain.

No panicking. I might need all the extra air I can get. Hyperventilating isn't going to help.

Motts tried to call Vina, who didn't answer. She tried Nish next with a similar result. Teo, however, answered on the second ring. "I'm stuck in a freezer."

"What—"

"Teo?" Motts resisted the urge to fling her phone when the call was dropped. She'd lost what little signal she had. "Bugger."

Is now the time to panic?

Probably.

I am suddenly Ron Weasley.

Well, at least there aren't any spiders.

Changing tactics, Motts tried emergency

services, but the call didn't connect. She attempted to text almost every number in her phone. One of the messages had to reach them. She hoped.

Motts was cold. And beginning to slide from pretending to be calm straight into terrified. She banged her fists against the door and screamed her head off. "Is this soundproof?"

Do I want whoever shoved me to come in here and finish the job faster? Vina will notice; surely she will.

Rubbing her hands over her arms, Motts considered her options. None, really. She wasn't equipped to escape a freezer. *Why can't I remember what Nish said about these things?*

How long does it take for hypothermia to set in?

Keep moving.

Or should I stay still to save oxygen?

What's the best way to not die?

"This is the worst escape room ever." Motts had progressed from mild shivering to her teeth chattering so violently, she worried about cracking a tooth. "So cold."

I should text Teo.

Did I text him?

No, I called him.

It was hard to hold on to a thought. Motts tried four times to unlock her phone before finally getting the sequence right. No signal. She shifted around the icy room, hoping to find at least one bar of service.

She had no luck.

Returning to the door, Motts had run out of ideas. She kicked the hard metal again until her foot hurt. No amount of screaming brought a response other than making her throat sore and her head ache.

Heat rises. Don't sit on the floor. Why am I so tired? Maybe I should add survival videos to my YouTube playlist. Can you start a fire with frozen fish? I won't starve.

Wait.

Can I get food poisoning from eating a fishsicle?

As Motts tried to find a way to warm herself, she was bombarded by sound and light. She blinked in confusion at the change. Teo stepped into the room, pausing when he spotted her to his right.

"What?" Motts tried to form a full sentence, but her mind and mouth refused to cooperate. "Cold."

Teo grabbed a blanket Vina held out to him. He wrapped it gently around her. "Can you walk?"

"Sure." Motts tripped over her own feet trying to take a step. "No."

With exaggerated care, Teo lifted her into his

arms. He carried her past Vina. Motts noticed the O'Connells being spoken to by Perry and Hughie.

Teo bundled her into the passenger seat of his car. She was immediately hit by warm air blasting from the vent. "How are you feeling?

Motts couldn't stop shivering even with the fluffy blanket and warm air. Her head felt so fuzzy. "Cold. Home."

"Inspector Ash and Constable Stone can handle the questioning here for now. River's already at your cottage. We'll have the doctor meet us there. I imagine a cosy fire and more blankets will help." Teo practically threw himself into the vehicle. He slammed his door and jabbed the seat belt buckle a few times until it caught. "When you're warm again, you're going to tell me what happened."

Motts rested her head against the window, staring unseeing at the village. "Not supposed to drive on the streets in summer."

"I'm a detective inspector. I'll drive on water if I have to."

"Do you need a special dispensation from the pope to drive on water?" Motts clutched the blanket more tightly around her. "Dispensation. Dis. Pen. Sa. Tion. Good word. It would make a great alliteration. What are good *d* words?"

"Let's just get you home."

On the short drive to her cottage, Motts didn't stop shivering. Teo jacked the heat all the way up. It didn't manage to take the edge of the cold.

Teo pulled up behind River's car where it was parked outside the cottage. "Your friends have been texting each other. I believe your cousin is warming things up inside."

"Cold."

"I know." Teo helped her out of the car and into the cottage. "You'll be warm in no time."

"Motts." River glanced over from where he was stoking the fire. He had blankets piled on the coffee table. "I've got the kettle boiling. My hot chocolate isn't as brilliant as your dad's, but it'll do."

Teo gently helped her into the old armchair by the fireplace. He worked with River to wrap her up with all the blankets. "You're safe now. Can you tell me why you went into the walk-in freezer?"

"Someone punched me in the back." Motts shivered under her mountain of blankets. "Pushed me into the freezer. Slammed the door on me. I didn't voluntarily go inside."

"Did they?" Teo stood up, suddenly seeming taller and more intimidating. He grabbed River by the arm. "Doctor will be here soon. Stay with your cousin."

"Teo?" Motts was confused by the sudden thunderous expression on his face.

"I believe I'll help Detective Inspector Ash question the O'Connells."

Motts stared at Teo, who nodded, spun around, and strode purposefully out of the cottage. She turned to River, who grinned. "What?"

"Someone's getting their arse kicked." He sat on the edge of the armchair, helping Cactus over onto the blanket mound. "So, you know how you sent text messages to everyone in your phone?"

"Oh, no."

"I imagine your parents and mine will be here shortly. I tried messaging everyone to say you were okay, but mums will be mums." River patted her blanket-covered arm. "I imagine the kettle will be boiling shortly."

"Can't you text my parents to stay away?"

"I'd take a bullet for you, but your mum is terrifying." River disappeared into the kitchen. He came back several minutes later with a mug of hot chocolate. "If you're wondering what happened, Vina noticed you'd gone missing. She spoke with Teo, who'd apparently gotten a call from you. He raced over with Perry and Hughie. Nish phoned me to come up to the cottage and prepare to defrost you."

"I'm not frozen minced meat."

"You will be when your mum gets here." He sat on the coffee table across from her. "You scared me half to death."

Motts clutched the mug and soaked up the heat. "Still not frozen minced meat."

By late afternoon, Motts almost regretted being rescued. The walk-in freezer might've been cold, but at least it was quiet. Her family and friends had descended on her cottage along with the doctor and two police officers.

The doctor had left rather quickly after determining Motts just needed to continue to warm up. She hadn't been in the freezer long enough to do permanent damage. The news hadn't done anything to calm her mum down.

"This is what happens when you move to Cornwall," her mum huffed at her. She dislodged the comforting arm Motts's dad tried to wrap around her. "Not now, dear. She needs soup."

"Soup? And what happens when you move to Cornwall?" Motts stared at her mum over the mound of blankets. "Getting locked in a freezer? Is it a regional issue? Are people frequently being pushed inside frozen tombs? Freezing fears fiercely froze follicles."

"Follicles?" River teased.

"Fossils? Fronds? Frogs?" Motts couldn't think of a better word to end her alliteration. "Friends."

"I'm not sure your mum finds this as funny as we do." He'd stayed close by, shielding her a little from the onslaught of parental concern. "Why are you poking me?"

"Time to peel off a few of these layers and douse the fire." Motts had definitely defrosted. She nudged River. "I've gone from frozen to melting in a sauna. Give me a hand. I feel like a sweaty mummy at this point."

With help from both River and Vina, Motts unwound the layers of blankets from around her. She hadn't even known she owned so many. Some of them must've been her auntie Daisy's; her cousin probably dug into the linen closet upstairs to find them.

"The mums are fighting." Vina squished into the armchair with Motts once the blankets had been removed. She nodded toward the kitchen where Motts's mum, her auntie Lily, and Leena were in a heated debate. "They can't agree on what sort of supper will warm your cockles."

"Warm my cockles?" Motts shoved Vina off her armchair. "Think we can sneak out and grab a pizza? I'm not hurt."

"You suffered trauma." Vina flicked her on the knee. "Don't you want to be coddled?"

"No, I want to know who pushed me into a freezer, so I can...." Motts hesitated. She didn't handle confrontation well. "I'll think of something."

"If we're going to get takeaway, we'll need to be sneaky." River crouched down next to the chair. "What if we say Teo needs you to give an official statement? We'll hop in my car. Nish can meet us at the Buccaneer. That'd get us the pizza you want along with kebabs and chips."

"You two were never the sneakiest of children." Her granddad crept up behind her chair. He leaned over to tap his grandson on the head. "Why don't you three head out? Your gran and I will run inter-ference with the fearsome mums. Escape while you can."

Picking up Cactus and fitting his walking harness on him, Motts carried him out with them. Being outside and holding her purring cat, she felt some of the knots in her release. The parental chaos in the cottage had made processing everything impossible.

"Nish will pick up the pizza. I believe your Teo agreed to grab drinks and some sort of dessert for us." River waited until they'd crowded into his car. "We'll go to Talland Bay. Still nice enough out to enjoy the sunset on the beach. We can eat and chat. Let the grandparents calm the waters at your cottage for us."

Motts cuddled with Cactus in the back seat. She rested her head against the window. "No shouting."

"When do I ever shout?" River glanced at her in the rear-view mirror. "We'll be extra quiet. I promise."

Chapter Seventeen

WAKING UP EXHAUSTED AFTER A SERIES OF nightmares, Motts drowned her sorrows in a strong cup of coffee and a few slices of toast. She added so much lemon curd that she thought her lips might pucker off her face from the tartness. The bright, sugary spread helped wake her up and chase the dreams away.

Her mind kept trying to drift back to yesterday and her close call with a frosty end. On the plus side, her parents were spending the day with her grandparents, who lived next door to her uncle and auntie. Granny Martha could run circles around her daughter-in-law.

Granny Martha had always encouraged her two

grandchildren to fly as high as they wanted. She'd been one of the reasons Motts had the courage to pursue running her own business. *I should visit with them more often. I'm a dreadful granddaughter.*

The reprieve would be brief, however. Her mum definitely hadn't got the "Cornwall isn't safe" lecture out of her system yet. It didn't matter to Motts, who had no intentions of leaving her cosy cottage by the sea.

Motts took her laptop, Cactus and Moss, and her tea out into the garden. She allowed them to explore the garden while she considered her plan for the day. "What will you do if you actually catch the butterfly?"

Meow.

"Helpful."

"Are you in the garden, poppet?"

Motts shut her laptop and darted around Cactus to open the garden gate for her granddad. John Mottley had run a bookshop in Looe for years before selling it. He'd met his beloved wife Martha in the library at university. They loved telling that story to their grandkids. "Did you leave Gran to fend for herself?"

"My Martha never once backed down from a

fight." He gave her a fierce hug before slowly bending down to greet Cactus. "Hello, young man. Taking care of my granddaughter, are you?"

"Granddad."

"Now don't go getting yourself addicted to catnip and stumbling around the village. You'll make a name for yourself in the wrong way." He continued to lecture Cactus, who purred up a storm.

"*Granddad.*"

"What are your plans for the day?" He wandered around the garden, inspecting her growing plants with Cactus on his heels. "Your lemon verbena needs pruning. Why don't I come over on the weekend next to help you out? Your gran's going on one of her trips again."

At least twice a year, Motts's grandmother went on a driving tour with several of her friends. Her granddad always stayed home. He tended to spend most of the time either reading or with his grandkids.

Motts shared both her love of gardening and her allergies with her granddad. "I've been thinking about adding a trellis along the fence later this summer. I want to try my hand at growing peas."

"You'll want to plant them either this autumn or

next spring. Give them the best chance at growing." He inspected the area of the garden she'd pointed out. "I might have wire netting you could use. I'll bring some over when I come to help with your pruning. You can store it in the shed until you're ready to plant. Now, what are your plans for the day? Hmm?"

"I've got three more paper columbines to fold and add to an arrangement for one of Marnie's brides. It'll take me a minute." Motts retrieved Moss and gestured for her granddad to lead Cactus into the cottage. "After I drop the flowers off at the bridal shop, I wanted to...."

"You wanted to?" He followed her over to the table where her origami papers were laid out. "Were you going to continue your investigation? Maybe poke the O'Connells with a stick? See which of them murdered Nadine?"

Motts studiously kept her attention on folding the last few columbines. "Did you know Nadine O'Connell?"

"Your gran knew her better. I knew her husband and her son-in-law a little. Can't say I liked any of them. Nadine could test the patience of a saint, as they say." He picked up one of the flowers to inspect. "I do remember how much she butted heads with

Amy even back when she was a young girl. Those two never got along."

"Mother and daughter?"

"Amy was a troubled soul." He shook his head, then offered the flower back to her. "They had vicious rows before Nadine fell ill. When your gran told me Amy planned to care for her mother, you could've blown me over with a cotton swab."

"How do you blow someone over with a cotton swab?"

"With great care and attention to detail."

Motts finished up the last of the flowers. She decided not to attempt to figure out what he meant. "Could Amy kill her own mother?"

"Almost everyone is capable of murder under the right conditions. Amy had a temper for sure. I doubt an extended illness improved either her or Nadine's personality." He absently patted Cactus on the head. "My money is one of the boys. I don't see how Amy could've carried her mother out to sea."

"Jasper and Mikey." Motts had the former on the top of her list. "Jasper definitely inherited his mum's temperament."

"I've been thinking about using a cold storage—"

"For what?" Motts carefully completed her bouquet and tried not to laugh at the absurdity of her granddad renting a cold storage. "What are you going to put in there?"

"Fish?"

"You always give the fish you catch to Auntie Lily. Also, shouldn't you be discouraging my curious nature?" Motts gingerly attached one of the columbines to a paper-wrapped wire stem.

"The best part of being a grandparent is not concerning myself with parental restraints." He wiggled his bushy grey eyebrows at her, making her laugh. "And my job is to always encourage my grand-children."

"Courage cautiously calls comfortably casual constraints." Motts wrinkled her nose. "I ran out of c words."

"Come on then. We'll walk down to the village. We can run your errands, poke our nose in at the O'Connell warehouse, and still have time for lunch." He set Cactus down on the table. "And your nan isn't here to complain when I have a pint with my lunch."

"She'll know."

"And that's half the fun." He waited patiently while she finished the bouquet. "Will you carry it like that?"

"Could you grab the hatbox on the shelf behind you, please?" Motts used a sturdy box pilfered from

Marnie's shop. "This should keep the bouquet safe until we drop it off at the bridal shop."

"Well, come along, poppet. Adventure and my midday pint are just around the corner." Her granddad headed out of the cottage. He waited patiently while she topped up water and food for Moss and Cactus, then locked up and set her security system. "Good lad, your Teo. Like the cameras and alarm he's installed for you."

They left her granddad's car parked outside of her home and walked down the narrow steps into the village centre. After dropping off the flowers, Motts waved to a busy Marnie and meandered down the street toward the harbour. Her granddad told familiar stories about Polperro.

"What was dating Gran like?" Motts interrupted his retelling of one of his favourite fishing trips in his twenties.

"Being on a roller-coaster ride through candyfloss."

Motts considered the visual for a few seconds in silence. "Sounds sticky."

He coughed a few times and chuckled. "Does it?"

"The candyfloss. It dissolves. You'd get it in your face and eyes." Motts frowned at her granddad in confusion when he continued to laugh. "What?"

"Never mind, poppet."

"I've missed something, haven't I? Not sure I want to know." Motts sighed. She hated not understanding jokes. They continued up the lane until they reached the warehouse. She noticed a familiar vehicle parked in front. "Why is Teo here?"

Teo seemed to have the same question for her. He seemed utterly unimpressed with their presence outside the warehouse. Motts wasn't certain, though. "What are you doing? Aren't you supposed to be recovering at home and staying safe?"

"Granddad needs cold storage." Motts grabbed his arm and dragged him forward. "See? Granddad."

Teo folded his arms across his chest, glaring down at both of them. "For what?"

"Candyfloss." Motts paused, then rubbed her forehead while both men laughed. "You've met my granddad, right? At my auntie and uncle's house."

The two men shook hands while continuing to chuckle. With a Teo-sized impediment to poking their noses into the O'Connell business, Motts figured they might as well leave the police to their investigation. Her granddad, ever the social butterfly, invited the detective inspector to join them for lunch.

"Why don't I meet you there?" Teo agreed. "It won't take me long to wrap up here."

Her granddad wrapped his arm around her shoulders, leading her away from the warehouse. "Nice lad."

"Lad?" Motts shook her head. "We wasted a walk."

Wasted walk weighs... what's another w *word?*

"On the contrary, poppet, we'll have a lovely lunch. Your copper will join us. And we can pop by to see Amy at her cottage afterwards without his knowledge." Her granddad patted her arm and winked at her. "He'll never be the wiser."

"I've been to the creepy house with the dolls. Not sure I want to inflict them on my dreams again." Motts shuddered. "Besides, I don't believe she'd welcome me to her cottage."

"I've a history with her parents. You let me do the talking." He gave her another wink then guided her toward Griffin Brews. "Why don't we have a coffee while we wait for your copper?"

"He's not mine, Granddad."

"Is he not?"

"We're only dating." Motts had never seen the need to rush into labelling a relationship in the early stages. She'd keep repeating it until people stopped asking. "We're still figuring each other out."

"I think he's yours whenever you're ready for him to be." He went in when she held the door for him. "You take your time, though, poppet. Make him wait."

"Granddad."

Chapter Eighteen

"Are you okay, poppet? You've gone all flushed." Her granddad paused on the steps above her. "You know your gran started having hot flashes quite young."

Motts yanked off her jumper, hoping the T-shirt underneath would be cooler. "I never knew that. Mum certainly doesn't talk about menopause."

"Think it runs in my Martha's side of the family. Her mum suffered the same way. Not the greatest thing to inherit." He waited patiently for her to be ready to continue up the stairs. "I remember your gran sleeping with a fan at night for a number of years. I had to use an extra blanket to keep from getting frostbitten toes."

"Granddad."

"Suffering for my love." He winked at her. "Are you ready to tackle Amy?"

"It would've been so much more useful to have hot flashes yesterday before I almost turned into a pineapple Sparkle." Motts tied her jumper around her waist. "I don't even like that kind of popsicle."

Continuing up toward the O'Connell home, Motts wondered if Amy would be more receptive. She hadn't seemed thrilled to see them the last time. And the incident at the warehouse likely hadn't improved matters.

Over lunch, Teo hadn't told them much about the investigation. He said they were looking into it in connection with the cold case. His only other admission was that the security cameras around the warehouse had magically stopped working right before she'd been shoved into the freezer.

Motts didn't believe in coincidences. "Do you think Amy will talk to us?"

"Talk? Or get shirty and shout at us?"

"Either."

"She might chat with me, owing to my relationship with her dad. She did better with him than her mum." Her granddad reached the top of the steps and came to a stop. Motts had been keeping her eyes on the stairs to keep from tripping and wound up going straight into the back of him. "Granddad."

"Young Michael. You're the spitting image of your granddad." He grabbed Mikey's hand, shaking vigorously while shifting enough to allow Motts to continue up the steps. "How's your mother doing? I was sorry to hear about your grandmother."

Mikey glanced over at Motts, who didn't shake his hand. "Heard you got stuck in one of the freezers. Dangerous things. You should be careful around them."

Motts stared at Mikey. Was he threatening her or genuinely showing concern? She didn't want to assume the worst. "I didn't stroll into the icebox of death on purpose. Someone shoved me into it. Is there a ghost at the warehouse? A rogue fish spirit who wants revenge for being eaten?"

"A rogue fish spirit?" Her granddad chuckled. "So, young Michael, did you punch my granddaughter to try to kill her?"

Mikey gaped at both of them. "What? Are you joking? I'd never. I wasn't even near the freezers."

"Hmm." Her granddad huffed. "She didn't punch herself in the back, did she? If not you, then who?

Your mum and brother were at the warehouse as well."

"Well, it wasn't sodding me, you old—"

"Hey now," Motts interrupted him. "Don't be rude to my granddad."

They glared at each other at the top of the steps for almost a full minute. Mikey cursed at them and stomped off. He shoved his way past to jog down the steps toward the village.

"Something we said?" Her granddad watched the fleeing O'Connell. "Shall we brave the mother, since we've conquered the son?"

"Not sure she'll be any more welcoming." Motts found Mikey's strong reaction strange. "Was he angry at the accusation out of guilt or because he's innocent?"

"I don't *think* he shoved you. Could be wrong." Her granddad scratched his jaw. "His shock seemed genuine enough."

"Did it?" Motts hadn't been able to tell. He'd appeared angry to her. "If he's innocent, it leaves Jasper or their mum, Amy."

"Jasper certainly has a temper." He nodded down to where they could still see Mikey in the distance. "All the O'Connells have one. Runs in the family.

Came from their great-grandfather. He was a brute of a man."

Motts wondered how much trouble the O'Connell brothers had gotten themselves into over the years. Tempers didn't tend to mean calm waters and trouble-free lives. She'd have to remember to ask Hughie if he'd arrested them in the past. "Did their dad have a temper as well?"

"Both their dad and granddad. Hard workers. Harder drinkers. Nadine handled the business on land while they stayed out at sea if they weren't in the pub." Her granddad shifted his attention from the village to down the street toward the cottage. "Seems such a long time ago, poppet. Your gran and I never saw much of them once Nadine fell ill. It's hard being around a bitter person all the time. Such a brittle and prickly personality."

"Amy or Nadine?"

"Both, to be honest."

"What the hell do you want? I told you never to come back here."

Motts spun away from her granddad and noticed Amy O'Connell screaming at a scruffy familiar figure. "What in the world is Ashby doing here?"

"Friend of yours?" he asked while they tried to

sneakily watch the drama unfold in front of them. "This is better than *Gogglebox*."

"What's *Gogglebox*?" Motts watched Ashby with a growing sense of suspicion. Why would he go near Amy after his supposed traumatic run-in with them? Weird. "Is it a telly thing?"

"Our lovely odd little poppet."

"I'm almost forty."

"And?" He shrugged. "I'll always see the tiny brunette who hid from her mum in my study. You sat behind my old chair, folding paper into frogs and birds. I had a menagerie lining my bookshelves."

"You snuck me Jammie Dodgers and bags of Monster Munch." Motts had always loved his study. It smelled strongly of old books and coffee. "I used to pretend I'd stowed away on a pirate ship and underneath your desk was one of the cabins."

"Not you again." Amy's screech broke into their moment of nostalgia. She'd spotted them and come speeding down the path. "Haven't you learnt to mind your sodding business by now?"

"Are you speaking to me, Amy O'Connell?" Her granddad frowned down his nose at Amy, who came to a sudden stop.

The shouting drew Ashby slightly closer to them. He blanched when Motts stepped to the side and into view. She frowned when he raced off in the opposite direction.

Weird. Very weird. Why is everyone behaving so strangely today?

And what on earth is Ashby doing arguing with Amy O'Connell when he made it seem as though he had no reason to ever be in Polperro again?

"Why don't we head home, poppet?" He suggested when Amy spun around, stormed back to her home, and slammed the door firmly shut. "We can sneak by Treleavens for an ice cream. We deserve a treat."

"My treat."

"What sort of granddad lets his only granddaughter pay for ice cream?" He shook his head with a wry chuckle.

"Does that mean if River was a girl you'd let me pay?"

"No." Her granddad gave her a confused look. "I'd still be paying."

Motts had a distinct feeling she'd put too much thought into his rhetorical question. "Have you tried their lemon meringue flavour?"

When in doubt, talk about ice cream flavours and not my ability to misunderstand regular conversation.

. . .

DESPITE HER GRANDMOTHER'S BEST EFFORTS, MOTTS'S mum refused to be distracted for more than a day. The morning after the curious incident at the O'Connell cottage, her parents descended on her after breakfast. Her dad smiled apologetically, gave her a hug, and disappeared into the garden to inspect her shed.

Why does he have to see the shed? It hasn't changed at all. He's observed it loads of times.

His absence left her mum free to unload her thoughts. And she did. Motts focused her attention on a new quilling project and allowed the words to flow around her without hearing them.

"Are you listening?"

Motts glanced up from where she'd been cutting strips of pastel-coloured paper. "Not really, no."

"What is this?" Her mum grabbed one of the pale pink pieces. "Crafting?"

"You know what quilling is, Mum. A client commissioned a piece of art for her four-year-old daughter. It's going to have a bicycle with flowers." Motts continued cutting the strips. She had loads to do before beginning the process of turning them into shapes and scrolls. "Is the lecture over?"

"We're heading home to London. A detective

there wants to speak with us about Jenny again. We hoped you'd come home with us."

"I am home." Motts cut sharply, completely messing up the strip of paper. She set the ruined sheet and scissors down on the table. "I love Cornwall. I can breathe here. Unlike London, where every moment outside the house suffocated me."

"Don't be dramatic, darling," her mum argued.

"I'm rarely dramatic. I'm quiet. Silent even when I shouldn't be." Motts shot to her feet, reaching back to keep the chair from falling over. "I want coffee. I'm going for coffee. I love you. You'll want to be on the road to London sooner rather than later to avoid traffic."

"Darling."

"This is my home." Motts rushed out of the cottage, barely remembering to grab her backpack by the door. "I should've kept my temper."

"Morning."

Motts lifted her hand to shield her eyes from the sun. She finally noticed the unmarked police car parked behind her parents' vehicle. "Teo?"

"I wanted to see how you were doing in person. I see your parents are still visiting." He strode up to her and placed a firm hand on her shoulder. "Everything okay?"

"Family stuff." Motts eyed Teo suspiciously. "Why would Detective Inspector Byrne ask my parents to return to London to ask them questions about Jenny?"

"I have no idea how the minds of fancy London detectives work."

"Teo."

Chapter Nineteen

With her parents gone, Motts had taken time to lower her stress. She spent almost the entire day working on the bicycle project. Cutting paper, scrolling it, then glueing it in an arranged pattern had a meditative quality to it.

She went late into the afternoon, only remembering to take breaks when Cactus meowed plaintively at her. Wrapping up her work for the moment, she felt so much better. Her shoulders had relaxed, releasing so much of the tension from the past few days.

Her friends had given her space. Vina had stopped by after the café closed to drop off a few treats for her supper, but she hadn't hung around.

Motts was almost teary-eyed at their understanding and respect for her needs.

Deciding to finish her day with a cosy evening, Motts made her favourite supper—a fresh herb-spiced omelette with a cheddar toastie. She curled up with Cactus in bed to eat and watch through a playlist of one of her favourite YouTube channels, Robert Welsh. She loved watching both him and his twin brother, James; their voices were so soothing.

Meow.

"No, I don't think either of us needs to know how to create a cut crease on my eyelid. He has a lovely voice, though." Motts settled into her pillow. "Tomorrow we'll see if we can track Ashby down."

Meow.

"Maybe I'll bring River with me again." She thought about calling Teo, but he'd want to speak with Ashby on his own. "We can share our information after. What does Vina always say? Better to ask for forgiveness than permission? Not sure it's true."

Then again, Vina had a fantastic ability to talk her way out of trouble. She'd done so at university loads of times. Motts had no such luck.

Reaching over to grab her phone from the night-stand, Motts messaged her cousin. He suggested going with Nish or Vina instead since he had a business meeting in the morning. The brewery was expanding outside of Cornwall for the first time, and negotiations were resting on his shoulders.

Even via text, River sounded terrified. Motts had no doubts he'd be successful. He promised to text her after the meeting.

Her second message went to Vina. The twins were both taking the day off. Their parents had decided to close the café for a day.

Drifting off to sleep, Motts kept thinking about the O'Connells. If Nadine had been such a dreadful person, maybe her daughter killed her. One cruel word too many had caused people to snap before.

Or had Mikey wanted her out of the way to gain control of the company? It still seemed odd that it hadn't gone to Amy. Or Jasper, since he was the one to work at the warehouse.

Why let Jasper run the warehouse?

Despite Motts wanting to cycle to Fowey, Nish insisted on driving. He arrived bright and early with Vina. They brought coffee and traybake.

Leena had made her steamed rice, coconut, and banana traditional dish into a traybake. It was delicious. Motts had several slices on the short trip to Fowey.

"Why doesn't she sell these in the café?" Motts

tried to resist the urge for a fourth slice. "You'd never keep them in stock."

"Mums. Who knows their minds?" Vina offered the container to her. "Want another one?"

"No." Motts nodded with a grin. "Wish she'd sell this. I'd have one every morning."

They made good time to Fowey, arriving in time to grab the ferry. Over the twenty-minute ride, Motts practised her questions for Callie. Vina wasn't the *most* helpful assistant. She laughed. Even when she didn't, it seemed like she was. Motts gave up and decided to hope for the best.

"Hello, you three."

"Where's your friend Ashby?" Motts ignored the sigh from Nish on her left and Vina's snickering on her right. "Sorry. I meant, hello, and how are you doing? Also, where's your friend Ashby?"

"Welcome to Motts's guide to small talk. Lesson one, always greet someone before interrogating them," Vina teased. She leant against the counter to smile at Callie. "Have you seen Ash around lately?"

"Not since yesterday. Came by in the evening, really upset." She scratched her head for a moment. "Lilith's out on another tour this morning. She spoke to him. I'll text her."

While Vina and Callie chatted about kayak

tours, Motts stepped outside for some air. She knew Vina hadn't meant anything with her joke. Her brain didn't always get the message.

"She wasn't laughing at you." Nish joined her, watching tourists walking across the street. "Just teasing."

"I know."

And she did.

"I imagine the trouble is that knowing intellectually and emotionally are two different things." Nish once again proved why she often went to him for help understanding the non-autistics in her life. "Want me to chat with her?"

"No," Motts responded immediately. "It'll make everything awkward and weird."

"If you two are done gossiping out here, Lillith suggested we try the Fowey Hall Walk. He planned to hike it today." Vina closed the shop door behind her. "Seems an easy trek for an experienced climber. How are we going to find him?"

"Walk the trail?" Motts had gone around the circular path around Fowey a number of times. It was a moderate walk that usually took her around three hours. "Did she know when he set out?"

"Why don't you two walk the path? And I can stay here, since he'll probably swing by at some point to see Callie." Vina smiled winningly. "We don't *all* need to walk for hours."

Motts exchanged a look with Nish when Vina vanished into the kayak shop. "That was obvious even to me."

"Walking isn't really her thing." Nish grabbed his phone and pulled up a map. "If he left from Fowey, I'd wager he's walking the circuit clockwise. Why don't we head the opposite direction? Take the ferry over to Polruan, heading up the path counter-clockwise."

"Meet him somewhere along the way?" Motts wanted to question him away from Callie. He might be more open. "Chase him down the trail?"

"Let's hope chasing won't be required. It'll be difficult to explain if someone calls the police." Nish made sure his vehicle was securely parked. "Ready?"

They grabbed water and went to catch the ferry back across to Polruan. Motts always appreciated Nish's ability to enjoy silence; small talk wasn't required. It helped her relax.

"Motts."

She glanced up when he gestured toward a familiar figure hanging out on the quay in Polruan, waiting for the ferry to dock. "Short walk."

"Let's hope he doesn't bolt before we can get off

the ferry." Nish led the way, allowing her to hide behind him. "Here's hoping he doesn't recognise me from coming into the café."

They managed to get off the ferry and over to Ashby without him disappearing. He frowned in confusion at Nish, and his scowl only deepened when he noticed Motts. *So, someone's not ecstatic to see me again. I wish River was here.*

"Fancy running into you again." Ashby surprisingly broke the silence first. "Sorry I couldn't stay the other day."

"Shame." Motts had forgotten all of the questions she'd practised. *Typical.* "Why were you arguing with Amy O'Connell?"

"She accused me of stealing."

"Three years ago. So why go by her cottage now? I'd stay far away from someone who accused me of theft." Motts glanced up at Nish. "It's weird, right? Not just me being me."

"Definitely on the odd side," Nish agreed readily. He pointed down the street toward one of the shops. "Why don't we head over to the tea shop? We can have tea and a snack while Ashby tells us what's going on."

"Mini quiche." Motts loved the small quiches they served. River had brought a box of them to her a few weeks ago. "Food makes everyone feel better."

"Randomly accurate statement." Nish moved to the other side of Ashby. They walked the short trip down the street to the tea shop. "Why don't we sit outside? Not too many people out at the moment."

They found an empty table, got their teas and a variety of quiches. Ashby didn't seem overly anxious to talk with them. He studiously ignored the questions Motts asked, keeping his mouth full to avoid responding.

When the next ferry arrived, Vina joined them. She'd be unable to suppress her curiosity. It didn't make Ashby any more talkative, unfortunately.

He managed to converse for twenty minutes, responding to questions, yet never quite giving them answers. Motts ripped her napkin into tiny pieces. She'd hoped to get some clarification.

"I have a feeling our day is about to become far more complicated than you thought." Nish brushed crumbs off his shirt.

Vina added, "I spy with my little eye someone whose name starts with a *P*."

"*P*?"

"Detective Inspector Ash. You're a long way from Polperro." Vina waved at the man while he crossed the road from where he'd parked his vehicle. "Hello, Hughie. Fancy seeing you as well."

"Why do I suddenly feel guilty?" Motts whispered to Nish. "I haven't done anything wrong."

"We're putting our noses into police business. I imagine that's a lecture we're about to receive." Nish watched Hughie lead Ashby away to the vehicle. Detective Inspector Ash stayed by their table. "Is he under arrest?"

"What are you three doing here?" Inspector Ash appeared more exasperated than genuinely annoyed, though Motts wasn't entirely sure. "And why are you chatting with our suspect?"

"Friendly people chat." Vina snagged the last bite of quiche from her brother's plate. "We're welcoming him to the area."

"The area? You're in Fowey." He turned away from the twins to focus on Motts. "Aren't you too close to this investigation already? Both myself and DI Herceg hoped you'd steer clear until we've made an arrest. We want you to stay safe."

"I'm having tea and quiche." Motts didn't understand why Vina started snickering. "What? I am? Perfectly safe occupation. What's dangerous about a mid-morning snack?"

"Elevenses," Nish interjected.

"More like second breakfast." Vina offered her own two cents.

"You're not hobbits." Inspector Ash peered over his shoulder at Hughie, who'd returned from securing their suspect. "I suppose he's at least part troll."

"I'm a friendly giant." Hughie made a point of standing as tall as possible to emphasise his height. "Did you three discover anything useful?"

"Constable." Inspector Ash sighed when the constable simply shrugged.

"Ashby had a heated conversation with Amy O'Connell the other day," Motts blurted. She blocked Vina's attempt to pinch her on the arm. "What? We're not *actually* detectives. They're the ones who can catch the killer."

Even if we have to help them along just a little.

Hughie crouched down next to Motts. "Teo's waiting for us at the station. He did want me to say he'll stop by to see you later."

Bugger.

"Somebody's in trouble," Vina teased.

Chapter Twenty

"WHY DO YOU THINK, CACTUS?" MOTTS HELD UP HER finished quilling piece. She'd spent a painstaking amount of time with tweezers and glue, adjusting the scrolls of paper into place. Of the various aspects, she'd found the finicky balloons above the bicycle to be the most difficult to get right. "Yes, it's bright and cheerful. Perfect for the birthday girl."

Despite Hughie's warning, Teo hadn't stopped by for either a friendly chat or an official lecture. She wondered if they'd cracked the case. Had Ashby been involved?

"Knock, knock."

"I'm taking your key away from you." Motts didn't shift her attention from gently packing up the framed artwork. "Since you're here, want to give me a lift? I need to deliver this to Plymouth."

"Plymouth?" River drooped dramatically against the kitchen counter. "It's an hour with good traffic. And when is traffic any good during the summer?"

"I'll buy you lunch at Toot." Motts dangled the carrot in front of her cousin's nose. He'd been going on about wanting to try the Persian restaurant for ages. "Falafel falls freely from...."

"Run out of *f* words?"

"You're not funny. Oh, there's one."

"Fine. I'll brave the traffic for a falafel. You're buying." He bent down to scratch Cactus behind the ear. "How about you? Want to go for a ride?"

"Probably best to leave him to guard the cottage." Motts knew Cactus wasn't overly thrilled with lengthy excursions in the vehicle. She'd tried having him ride in the basket of her bicycle once. Never again. They'd both been traumatised. "Can we go now? I've geared myself up for small talk with a client. Best to get it over with while I'm mentally prepared."

They miraculously hit just one mild traffic jam on the way to Plymouth. River had chosen to drive the shortest, most direct route. Motts was relieved when she managed to drop off the quilled art without having to use any of her practised conversation.

"So, falafels?" River chuckled when she practically melted with relief into the passenger seat. "Not as scary as you feared?"

"Falafels."

Sitting down for lunch at Toot, they got a sharing platter of starters. Motts particularly enjoyed freshly baked bread and houmous; River inhaled the cinnamon-flavoured ground lamb meatballs. The two barely had room for sticky, sweet baklava.

They made room.

Always room for dessert.

After eating way too much for an early lunch, they decided to return to Polperro. River had to get to work at the brewery. Motts had an afternoon in the garden planned out.

Weeds wouldn't pull themselves.

"River." Motts had noticed a familiar white van slipping in behind them when they went around the roundabout near Kernow Mill. "Coincidence. Right?"

"Do you believe in coincidences? Not sure I do." River gripped the steering wheel tightly. He kept glancing up at the rear-view mirror. "Definitely Jasper."

Motts tugged on her seat belt and then yanked down on the collar of her shirt. *Breathe. It's going to be fine. He couldn't have been waiting for us. No one knew where we were going.* "Should we call someone?"

"And tell them what? Jasper's following us? He'll tell them he's heading back home, which might be true." River sped up the vehicle. "We'll see if he keeps up with us."

He did.

"River."

"I see him." He bent forward slightly, his hands still holding too tight to the steering wheel. "Maybe he's trying to scare us."

"He's succeeding." Motts wondered if Amy had told her son about them coming by the cottage. Or had Mikey confronted his brother? "Speeding speedily."

"Short and succinct." River managed a tense smile. "You might send Hughie a message. See if our gentle troll will meet us at the top of the village."

On the surface, a commercial van driving on the road behind them shouldn't have induced fear. Motts knew they'd never be able to explain to the police. She couldn't quite calm her heart rate down.

Jasper revved his engine behind them. He sped

up enough to be practically riding on their bumper. His lights flashed at them while he honked his horn.

"Does he want us to pull over?" Motts wondered.

"I am not pulling over unless I see a police vehicle." River's voice shook. "We'll be fine."

"You sound like you're talking through a fan blade." She twisted in her seat to get a better view of the van behind them. "How is flashing his lights going to do anything? You're going over the speed limit, so that's not the issue."

Jasper's aggressive driving continued to escalate. The van edged closer and closer to them, despite River trying to increase the distance between the vehicles. Motts held her breath, expecting the hit anytime.

River cursed under his breath. He tried to overtake the person in front, but oncoming traffic forced him back into the lane. "Did Hughie respond to you yet?"

"No." Motts sent another text to the constable, one slightly more panicked and demanding. "Maybe he's got his phone turned off?"

All the way through the narrow two-lane roads, Jasper rode their bumper. Motts had never been so grateful to see the familiar curve that signalled the turn towards the village. She wondered what passing vehicles thought of the strange behaviour from the van.

Surely someone had noticed the aggressive driving.

"I don't understand why he's doing this." Motts's breath caught in her throat when stopped traffic drew her attention. She thrust her hand out instinctively as River slammed on his brakes. "Oh my god."

"Hold—"

A sudden screech of tires cut off River's warning. With the weight of his commercial van and how close they'd been, Jasper clearly couldn't stop in time. He swerved wildly into the opposite lane of traffic, tipping the van onto its side and sliding straight into them.

River threw his arm out in front of Motts, trying to protect her when the impact threw them both forward. "Sodding berk."

Motts was only capable of breathing.

And barely capable of doing that.

"Motts? Love?" River twisted in his seat, yanking his seat belt off. He reached a hand out to gently grasp her shoulder. "Are you okay?"

She heard him, yet her brain refused to formulate a response. It was like someone had shoved cotton into her ears. Everything sounded muffled, including her own thoughts.

"Easy, there. Try to slow your breathing." River ran his fingers gently across her shoulder and neck. "Does this hurt?"

Motts shook her head slowly. She tried to ignore the cacophony of sound beginning to pick up outside of their car. "Fine."

"You're not fine."

"Fine."

"Not actually fine." River unbuckled her seat belt. "We should get out of the car. Does your neck or back hurt?"

"Fine." Motts closed her eyes, trying to not only regulate her breathing but settle her mind. She had a feeling finding her words would be a good thing. "Fine."

I'm fine.

Fine.

Just fine.

Completely and totally not actually fine.

"I'm getting out of the car. You should stay here until paramedics arrive. I'm worried about your neck." River frowned when she reached for the door handle. "Motts."

"I'm fine." *Oh, look, I managed an extra word. Progress.*

Despite her cousin's protests, Motts climbed out of the vehicle. She whistled at the state of it. The entire back of his car had been crushed in by the force of the impact.

"Motts." River stepped around to stand in front of her. "It's like the scene in *Terminator*."

"What's a terminator?"

"Never mind. Oh, thank the copper gods."

"Copper gods? As in the metal or the police?" Motts was glad words were coming back. Now if the rest of her mind would focus, she might make sense of things and stop being unnecessarily pedantic. "I see Hughie."

Wandering away from the wreckage, Motts found a clear, dry spot of grass to sit down on. She wondered how long it would take for her mum to use the accident as yet another reason for her to move back to London. *Never going to happen.*

"I'm beginning to sense a trend." Hughie whistled while inspecting the damaged vehicles. He stepped to River. "We'll get a tow truck out for these. Neither of them's going to be driven out of here."

Leaving him to handle things, Motts assessed her injuries. *None.* She had a slight tenderness in her chest from the seat belt but nothing else. No twinges in her back or neck, thankfully.

"Paramedics should be here shortly. They're driving over from Looe. They'll want to check all of you out." Hughie ignored Motts's protests. He'd already had a brief chat with several of the witnesses. "You don't have to go to the hospital. Just let them assess the situation. Young Jasper claims he lost control."

"Jasper's not that young. And he did lose control." Motts didn't believe "lost control" fully described the accident. "He followed us practically all the way from Plymouth. Thought he was trying to run us off the road."

Hughie came over and crouched in front of her. He kept his voice down to avoid being heard by the others. "I've a decent case for reckless and aggressive driving against him. Not much else. I can't prove what caused him to follow too closely."

"Figures." Motts wrapped her arms around herself. "Can I go home now?"

"Not until the paramedics check you out," he insisted.

Whatever her misfortune, Motts had the singular good luck to escape serious injury no matter the situation. The paramedics deemed her to be fine. They weren't so sure about Jasper, given the violence of his crash.

"I'll wait for the tow truck. Dad's on his way to give me a lift. Why don't you have Hughie take you home?" River handed over her bag and the crushed container of food. "Not sure this is good for much now. Maybe compost? Cactus might like smashed scones."

"Cactus has standards." Motts glanced toward Constable Stone, who appeared busy. "I'll walk home."

"Motts."

"*River.*" She stared down her cousin. "I've had quite enough of cars for one day. I'll be perfectly safe walking through the village, given how crowded it is."

With the growing number of tourists exploring the village, Motts managed to sneak through to the narrow steps leading up the hill to her cottage. She'd been afraid Marnie or one of the Griffins would spot her. Closing the door on the world had never felt so good.

"I'm never going outside again. Ever." Motts rested against the locked door. She smiled down at Cactus, who rubbed against her leg and purred loudly. "Well, okay, maybe just for today we'll hide from everyone."

Meow.

"Yes, you do deserve a treat for keeping the house safe." She deserved one as well.

With tea made and a plate of biscuits along with a treat for Cactus, Motts ensconced herself in the chair by the window. She drew one of the blankets from the couch across her lap.

A quiet evening was not on the cards. Motts had sat down with her tea when her doorbell rang. She ignored it.

They'll go away.

They didn't. Ringing turned to knocking. Motts forced herself out of the comfortable armchair and blankets, trudged to the door, and yanked it open.

"Your hair is flat."

"Can we talk?" Callie's spiked hair was significantly squashed. She held up a gaudy necklace. The design seemed straight out of one of the costume dramas Motts's mum enjoyed watching. "It's about Ashby."

Tea had been made. Biscuits eaten. Motts held the rather heavy necklace with what appeared to be diamonds and rubies; she had no idea why.

"Gaudy goods grace girls' gowns." Motts

inspected the engraved word on the tag on the clasp. "NO."

"I believe it's N.O. Initials for—"

"Nadine O'Connell," Motts guessed. "Why do you have this?"

"Ash's bag." Callie shifted uncomfortably. She gulped down some of her tea. "Snooped when the cops picked him up. Couldn't help myself. It was underneath his pants along with a few other trinkets. I picked him up from the station yesterday. He hasn't noticed it missing so far."

"How? Hard to miss, given how heavy the thing is." Motts deftly shifted the necklace away from Cactus, who tried to swipe at one of the larger gems. "Police might want this for evidence. Why are you bringing this to me?"

"Makes him seem guilty." Callie pointed to the necklace. "You're investigating."

"Not an investigator," Motts grumbled. She knew Teo would want the necklace and likely believe Ashby had stolen it after killing Nadine. "Why did he keep it?"

"Ask him. I'm afraid he's going to tell me he killed her. I can't believe he's capable of murder." Callie shoved a biscuit into her mouth. She tapped her fingers against the side of her mug. "Can you talk to him?"

Motts knew what Teo and the other police would say. They'd tell her to refuse. Her curiosity, as always, got the best of her. "Is he at your place?"

Do I want to get in a car again?

No.

"Invite him here." Motts didn't want Ashby in her cottage, but going in a vehicle was even less attractive to her. "Tomorrow. It's been a day."

Promising to bring Ashby the next day, Callie left. Motts found a secure hiding spot for the necklace away from prying eyes and curious cats. She was washing the mugs when her doorbell rang. Again.

Motts dried her hands off on her jeans and went to see who was disturbing her peace this time. "Go away."

"Can I come in, please?" Mikey O'Connell reached out to stop her from slamming the door. "Please?"

"I've had quite enough of O'Connells for one day." Motts grabbed Cactus when he went to slip through the crack in the door. "What on earth could you possibly want?"

"Jasper...." Mikey trailed off when a vehicle could be heard coming up the lane. "Sod it."

Motts watched in complete bewilderment as he bolted away from her. He'd disappeared down the steps to the village by the time Teo parked in front of her cottage. "Hello. Please go away."

"I brought a sack of chips and a chocolate bar."

"Well, fine. Come in." Motts sighed. She set Cactus down so he could trot over to greet his favourite detective inspector. "Just don't be shouty."

"I'm never shouty." Teo lifted Cactus up onto his shoulder. "Were you hurt?"

"Perfectly fine. And you *look* like you're about to be shouty," Motts insisted. "Your eyebrows are all aggressively lowered over your eyes."

"Shouty isn't a word. And my eyebrows are always like this." Teo offered her the packet of chips while adjusting Cactus carefully on his shoulder. "Who'd you chase off down the stairs?"

"No one." Motts ignored him and checked all around the front of the cottage.

"What are you searching for?"

"A sign inviting everyone I've ever met into my cottage. I've never had so many visitors." She was being mildly dramatic, but it had been a day. "Did Hughie call you?"

"Inspector Ash and I heard the sirens heading out of the village. River told me you were there." Teo followed her into the cottage, shutting the door behind them. "I won't stay long. You should get some rest after your day. Just wanted to check in on you. Bring something to cheer you up."

Don't mention the necklace.

Don't mention the necklace.

I can tell him about the necklace tomorrow after we chat with Ashby.

"Necklace."

Bugger.

"Pardon?" Teo paused in the middle of putting the treats on the counter and dislodging Cactus from his shoulder.

"Thank you." Motts attempted a smile. She gave up and just tried not to frown. "I said, thank you."

It's a good thing I never tried to work in a job requiring secrecy.

I'd be pants at it.

Chapter Twenty-One

THE MORNING AFTER THE ACCIDENT, MOTTS WOKE UP feeling about a hundred years old. Her neck and back had tightened up, and she had an impressive bruised strip going across her front from the seat belt.

Motts wanted to hide from the world again. She knew from experience doing so would only make going out harder the next time. Like Moss, pulling into her shell and staying in the cottage for weeks on end wouldn't be healthy.

"Coffee. Coffee and a croissant." Motts carefully measured out Cactus's breakfast. She'd brave the outdoors to feed her cravings. And worst-case scenario, she could sneak into the kitchen at Griffin

Brews to eat. "Maybe Callie and Ashby can meet me there. Neutral territory."

Meow.

"I'm sure Leena will have treats for you." Motts rubbed his ears. "You behave yourself. Take care of Moss."

Meow.

"I hear the rain." Motts finished clearing out Moss's terrarium. She made sure Cactus's sleeping blanket on the windowsill was appropriately fluffed up. "I won't take too long. We can venture into the garden once it stops drizzling."

Motts grabbed her wellies, coat, and umbrella. She loved her rain boots. Vina had bought them for her on a shopping trip to London. They were the perfect shade of blue, with sailboats all around.

Stepping outside into the softly falling rain, Motts wandered up the path to look over the cliffs to the sea. Gloomy skies. Rough seas. Salty air. She loved walking outside during a gentle summer shower.

Tourists tended to stay indoors, for one. The downside of a steady drizzle was how slick the steps became. She carefully managed to get down the stairs into the village.

"Morning, dear." Doc waved from the doorway of the post office. "Enjoying the morning rain?"

Motts tilted her umbrella to see him. "It's lovely, isn't it?"

"Beautiful. If I were a young man, I'd be hiking the coastal path this morning. Nothing like a Cornish summer rain." He winked at her. "My Elys would want me to tell you not to catch your death of cold. So, there, I've said it. Now you run off and enjoy jumping in puddles on my behalf, since I can't."

In London, Motts had never gotten to know her neighbours. She'd been too afraid. Another reason she'd never move back to the big city.

"Hello, love." Marnie jogged across the street to walk beside her. She ducked under Motts's umbrella. "Rumour has it Amy O'Connell's turned on her sons. She suggested to your inspector that her Jasper and Mikey conspired. Conspired."

"Did she?" Motts stopped so suddenly Marnie kept going and had to turn around to come back. "Not surprised. What do you mean rumour has it?"

"Overheard my Perry chatting with Inspector Herceg last night." Marnie grinned. "Oh, must run, someone's outside the shop. Come by later."

Motts could only stare at the bridal shop owner in bemused silence. "Bye then."

Continuing down the street, Motts went around the corner and across to Griffin Brews. She smiled at Nish, who was writing out the daily specials in chalk on the board set up in the window. He pushed open the door for her.

"Morning." She accepted the quick hug from Nish. "How's River? He never texted me last night."

"Sore. Bruised. He's going in for a massage on his neck and back. His car is completely wrecked. Not sure they'll be able to fix the thing." Nish looped his arm around hers. "His mum brought over a boatload of food."

"Mums." Motts had no doubts Auntie Lily would keep a close eye on her only son. "I'm glad my mum hasn't heard about it yet. I'll never hear the end of how dangerous Cornwall can be."

"Trust Motts to venture out into the rain after being in a car accident." Vina stepped up to the counter. "Drop your brolly in the bucket by the door. No dripping on the floors. I've already mopped up once. No dripping."

Motts handed her umbrella and raincoat to Nish when he held his hands out. She frowned when both Vina and Nish broke into giggles. "I won't ask. I already know whatever made you two cackle like hyenas is either gross or sexual. Maybe both."

"Mum and Nish made a new flavour." Vina wisely changed the subject. "Cardamom and caramel latte. It's almost like a spiced brown sugar coffee with cream. Delish."

"Perfect on a rainy day. We'd planned to keep it for autumn, but today's a brilliant day for it." Nish slipped behind the counter to make a large mug for her. "We've also got a batch of salted pistachio and chocolate croissants."

"You'll want several. Trust me." Vina plated up three of them. "Your usual table or the one in the kitchen?"

"Usual. For now." Motts retreated to the round table in the far corner of the café. "Callie and Ashby might be joining me later."

"Oh?" Vina lifted one perfectly sculpted eyebrow. "Are they? Why?"

"Mysterious metals mingled." Motts bit into her first croissant. "Magnificent."

"None of those words make sense together. But I'll take the compliment on my creation." Vina preened.

"Callie brought me a piece of intrigue last night." Motts finished chewing, brushed her fingers on a napkin, and pulled her phone out to show Vina the image of the necklace. She scrolled over to the close-up of the clasp. "Think it might've been Nadine O'Connell's."

"How did Callie get a gaudy bit of jewellery from Nadine O'Connell?" Nish peered over Vina's shoulder down at the photo. "Ashby?"

"Got it in one." Motts pointed at her nose. She grabbed for a second croissant. "These are going to sell like hotcakes."

"Teo and Perry have been stopping by in the mornings for coffee. Think they're working on the O'Connell case together. Innis saw them by the harbour and warehouse yesterday." Nish got on with the owner of the fish shop better than Motts. "He's keeping an eye out. I'll try to distract them if they pop in. You know Teo will have questions if he sees you chatting with one of his suspects."

Motts had no doubt Teo would find her presence at a table with Ashby suspicious. "I'll tell him about the necklace. Eventually."

While the twins returned to preparing for the morning rush, Motts eased her tablet out of her backpack. She wanted to make a few design notes for a new commission. She'd received a few emails from potential clients and wanted to get a head start on her ideas for them.

One of the messages had come from a friend of

Marnie who'd wanted to remain anonymous. Strange, but Motts trusted Marnie. The person wanted a bouquet of peonies in a shadowbox frame.

Since her bouquets tended to be made of origami, Motts wanted the quilling work of peonies to be special. The messages had indicated the piece was a memorial for a beloved family member who had passed away. It had to be perfect.

"Mottsy."

Motts lifted her head up slowly, struggling to switch her mind from creative mode to the real world. Vina waited patiently by her table. "What?"

"Your guests are here. I'll bring you another coffee in a second." Vina picked up the empty mug and plate. "Want another croissant?"

"Sure. You'll bring them mid-conversation to satisfy your curiosity." Motts knew her best friend well. "Croissants."

"Yes, croissants," Vina promised.

While Ashby and Callie got their order, Motts sat waiting. Anxiety built. She shoved her hands into her pockets to keep from scratching her palms raw.

"Morning." Callie slipped into one of the seats around the small table while Ashby took the other. "I haven't been here early in the mornings. I'm usually working or in a kayak at this time."

Small talk.

Motts nodded. *Why did I think I could manage this? I should've made Vina sit with me.* "Right."

"Well, we've covered the awkward greeting." Callie stirred her coffee absently. She hadn't taken a sip or touched her breakfast pasty. "Ash. You wanted to get the truth off your chest. Why don't you start? We don't need to hem and haw around how our day is going."

"I...." He stared morosely down at his cup of tea. "She asked me to sell the necklace for her."

"She?" Motts found the explanation far too simple and also impossible to prove. "I assume you mean the elder Mrs O'Connell."

"Nadine. I used to camp in her garden on my hiking trips across Cornwall when she was healthy. Amy accused me of taking advantage of her mother. Tossed me out on my ear." Ashby's fingers curled around the handle of the cup tightly. "Poor old woman. She reminded me of my gran. I don't care what anyone else says. She was always kind to me. I tried to help her. She wanted to hire a solicitor, for some reason."

"A solicitor? Why give you a necklace, though?" Motts knew Amy could be vile, mistrusting, and possibly dangerous. She still wasn't sure if she believed Ashby. "Why keep the necklace?"

"She went missing. Not two days after I saw her. I was frightened." He shoved the tea away, causing it to slosh onto the table. He swiped at the mess with a napkin. "What would I tell the police? I've got this expensive jewellery from an elderly woman who's disappeared? They'd never take my word for it. I had no proof."

Not sure I believe you now.

Then again, if he killed her for it, why not sell the necklace?

"Do you not have any evidence at all? A text message or something?" Callie clearly had some of the same reservations as Motts. "What did the police say when they questioned you earlier in the week?"

"I didn't tell them." Ashby gathered up the soggy napkins. He twisted around, looking for a rubbish bin, and froze. "They won't believe me."

Before either Motts or Callie could respond, Ashby had rushed away from the table. He fled the café. The two women stared after him in silence.

"He does that a lot." Motts noticed two familiar faces by the door. Ashby had obviously spotted the two detective inspectors and been scared. "Bugger."

While Perry Ash queued up in the line by the

counter, Teo headed directly toward her table. Motts shifted in the chair. She smiled when Vina popped over with a refill.

A distraction, a blatant attempt to eavesdrop, and a show of support.

"Well, I have a kayak tour to run. I better get home to Fowey." Callie downed her coffee, snatched up the rest of her pasty, and fled out of the café.

Motts glanced from the now closed front door to Teo to Vina. *Small talk. I can do this.* "Good morning. Fancy meeting you here."

"Motts." Vina snickered.

"What? They say that in movies." Motts pocketed her phone and put her tablet away. "I've been enjoying a rainy day and a cup of coffee. You should try the croissants."

See.

I can do small talk.

Teo stared Vina down until she backed away from the table with a quick wave to Motts. His attention turned fully to Motts. "Why don't you tell me about Ashby? And about the necklace?"

"Bugger."

Chapter Twenty-Two

"Right. Nish and I are dying from anticipation. You've been silent for a full five minutes." Vina made a show of topping of Motts's mug despite it being full. "Necklace. Mystery. Dedicated inspector versus casual amateur investigator. And go."

"Go where?" Motts hadn't intended to leave without finishing her croissant. "Oh, wait, you mean talk."

Vina tapped Motts on the shoulder gently. "Yes. Chat it up with your detective inspector. Confession is good for the soul, but do it so we can hear you because we're nosy."

Nish cleared his throat loudly.

"Fine. I'm nosy," Vina corrected.

"We're so sorry. She takes after her father." Leena

retrieved her daughter, pushing her across the room to the counter. "Enjoy your breakfast."

Teo watched the mother and daughter, who were having a heated whispered conversation. "Amy O'Connell suggested your friend Ashby stole from her mother and murdered her to keep her silent."

"Of course she did," Motts grumbled. "Ashby didn't murder anyone."

"Based on?"

She hesitated, stirring her latte. "I'm not sure."

"Morning, Ms Mottley." Inspector Ash settled himself at the table with them. He slid a mug and plate across to Teo. "How are you doing after the accident?"

"A little sore." Motts hoped the diagonal bruise across her upper body healed quickly. "I'll admit to not being anxious to ride in a car anytime soon."

"My Marnie wanted me to make sure you were doing okay." He offered comfort in his quietly stoic sort of way. "Was that our suspect sitting with you?"

Motts could understand how Perry Ash made detective inspector. He didn't have Teo's intensity, yet his quiet sternness was equally effective. "Ashby's aura aligns anxiously."

"Did it? I'm sensing yours is as well." Teo's lips twitched, and he took a sip of coffee.

The problem with facing two detective inspectors was Motts found Ashby's story suddenly even harder to believe in the retelling. He got a necklace from an elderly, infirm woman who wanted to escape her daughter. And kept it when she died.

It sounded so absolutely absurd. Yet, Motts believed him. She didn't know if either of the detective inspectors would be sold by her argument.

"Croissants." Motts brightened when Vina snuck over to drop one last breakfast pastry on her plate. "You're my favourite."

"Enjoy your breakfast." Vina rolled her eyes. She narrowed her gaze on the two inspectors seated at the table with Motts. "Play nicely, gentlemen. Interrogation is bad for the digestive system."

Motts smothered her laughter behind her latte. She didn't think either man expected to be warned off by the svelte and stylish Vina. "She's not wrong. Intense conversation can lead to indigestion."

"I'm sure we'll survive," Teo countered. "Why don't you let us decide for ourselves if we believe the tall tale?"

Pursuing her lips at the "tall tale" comment, Motts considered her options. She pressed on with telling what little she knew of Ashby's connection to the O'Connells. Even in the retelling, it sounded unbelievable.

And yet, still, she found herself even more convinced.

"She asked him to sell her necklace?" Inspector Ash definitely wasn't convinced. Motts didn't need to understand either tone or body language to see his incredulity. "Likely story."

"If he'd stolen it, why didn't he sell it the first chance he got? Three years now he's hung on to a valuable piece of jewellery," Motts pointed out. She'd showed the detective inspectors the photo of the necklace currently hidden inside her cottage. "It's incriminating evidence. If he'd killed her, getting rid of it should've been a top priority."

"Criminals, in my experience, don't often think logically or intelligently." Teo handed her phone back to her. "Why don't we head up to your cottage to retrieve the necklace? We're going to need to log this into evidence."

He means against Ashby.

How do I convince them he's innocent?

Am I convinced he's innocent?

Lost in thought, Motts didn't even notice Nish had bagged up her last croissant for her until she spotted the paper sack in front of her. The twins were way too good to her. She always felt grateful for her best friends, who treated her like family.

"Are you—" Teo cut off his question when Motts's phone began to go berserk. "Your alarm."

Motts grabbed her phone, fumbling to get the alarm turned off. "My cottage. Maybe it's a false alarm?"

The two detectives both stared at her. Motts shifted uncomfortably. They obviously didn't think it was a false alarm.

Their short trip up to the cottage seemed like hours. Motts's heart began to race when she spotted her front door. Teo grabbed her to keep her from racing inside.

"Cactus. Moss."

"We need to make sure no one's inside." Teo left her with Inspector Ash while he went into the cottage.

"I don't care about the poxy necklace. What about my family?" Motts tried to see into the hall-way. "Cactus?"

Meow.

Oh, thank everything. Thank all of your nine lives.

"Cactus." Motts's voice trembled. She latched on to her cat, who'd sauntered out of the open cottage door. "He's got something on his paws. Oh my. Is this blood?"

Inspector Ash jogged over to her. He gently lifted one of Cactus's paws. "I'd say he gave someone a good scratch. We're going to want to get a swab of this. Don't let him lick himself clean."

"I've got the alarm turned off." Teo joined them. "I've got a call in to a locksmith to fix your door. Nothing else is damaged. Where'd you hide the necklace?"

Motts gently handed Cactus over to Teo. She went straight into the cottage and retrieved the necklace. She offered it to Inspector Ash, who secured it in an evidence bag. "What about my cameras?"

"The company checked the footage for me. We've got a figure in a hoodie, face completely covered. I'll analyse it more thoroughly later." Teo had a careful hold on Cactus's paws. "Your hallway is a mess. I'd say they encountered your brave cat and decided not to press on further into the cottage."

Meow.

"Yes, you do deserve all the treats. We'll get you a nice big plate of tuna," Motts promised.

The technician arrived in impressive time to swab both of Cactus's front paws. He eyed the woman suspiciously but submitted to the inspection. Motts thought he did better than she would've.

"I'll get you all cleaned up." Motts left the police to chat. She wandered into her cottage, since they'd finished taking photos and fingerprints. "What a mess."

The hall table had been knocked over, a painting was off the wall, her coats and umbrellas were strewn across the floor.

Nothing seemed broken, at least.

"Can I help?" Teo offered. "Perry's got the CCTV footage from the security company. He'll take a closer look. The lab tech's off with the evidence. I'm hanging around for a bit. Just in case."

"In case they come back?" Motts carried Cactus through the mess in the front into the kitchen. "Let's get you cleaned up."

Meow.

"I know. You're a grand Celtic warrior. You're still having a bath." She gently washed off the blood from his paws, checking him over for any injuries. "Why don't I set you up with a nice snack by the window? You and Moss can gossip about what a brave boy you are."

With Cactus taken care of, Motts returned to the hallway. She leaned against the wall and stared at the mess. The security system was supposed to be a deterrent.

Some deterrent.

My poor painting.

Motts bent down to touch the frame. She shook her head, breathing in and out rapidly. Teo stepped up behind her and lifted the artwork to place on the wall.

"Why don't you join Cactus and Moss in the living room? Have some tea?" he suggested. He sighed when Motts shook her head. "How can I help?"

Go away.

Motts wanted to resettle into the cottage. She needed familiarity to wash away the sense of having her safest space violated, even if only briefly. "I need some quiet and space."

Teo eased back after righting the coat stand. "I'll speak with Perry. We'll see if Constable Stone can keep an eye on your cottage today."

"Teo."

He waved off her attempt to apologise. "Clear your head. I'll ask Nish to bring you a takeaway. Fish and chips are good for the soul, I'm told."

Motts managed a smile. She put the hallway table back against the wall and began replacing the items that had fallen off. "They are. Salty, vinegary chips. A greasy boon to a weary soul."

He chuckled, finishing placing the last coat on the stand. "There. All fixed up."

After Teo left, Motts closed the door. She unlocked and locked it a few more times, just to be sure. The hallway had returned to normal; nothing seemed out of place.

"What are you?" Motts spotted something poking out from underneath the rug. She eased out a receipt from the Griffin Brews. "Coffee and a pasty. Same as Ashby."

And likely the same order as twenty other people who came into the café. The receipt showed no identifying information. *Bugger. I'll text a photo to Teo later. And to Nish; maybe he can identify it for me—and the police.*

Later, when my head isn't buzzing from adrenaline and stress.

One of Motts's favourite things in the world was organising her supplies. She set multiple containers of papers on the coffee table. The peony project needed more work; she wanted a clear head before starting.

Meow.

"I know you're trying to be helpful. The last time

you did, I had to throw away an entire bouquet because you taught it a lesson." Motts gently plucked Cactus off the table and set him on the couch behind her. "You can supervise from a distance."

Meow.

"You'll survive the trauma of being separated from the coffee table." Motts grabbed the first container. She pried off the lid and began lifting out stacks of loose paper and organising them into piles based on colour and stack. "We'll survive."

No matter what.

Oh, this is a lovely purple. Maybe I can make a bouquet of irises for Teo's mum.

Chapter Twenty-Three

"Knock, knock."

"Why do you bother pretending to knock when you use your key? Better question. Why did I give you access to my cottage when you swan in as if it's yours?" Motts stared over the rim of her coffee mug at her cousin. He held up a Tupperware container. "Breakfast?"

"Mum made English breakfast baos. She insisted I bring them over and make sure you were okay." River peeled the lid off the container. Motts immediately grabbed one of the steamed buns. "Bacon, eggs, a stewed tomato sort of sauce. Works surprisingly well in the baozi."

Motts took a large bite of her bun. It tasted almost orgasmic, based on Vina's far too graphic explanation of one. She made up a mug of coffee for her cousin while they munched on the baos.

"Want to watch CCTV footage with me?" Motts had collected the video from the cameras in her cottage and planned to peruse it over breakfast. She might spot something the police hadn't. "Maybe you'll recognise the person if I don't."

Coffee and baos in hand, they sat beside each other at the kitchen table. Motts set up her laptop for them both to see. She queued up the video from the front of the cottage and hit Play.

"Here we go. Now, who's this berk." River leaned in closer to the screen. "Could be any bloke in a hoodie, to be honest."

"Where does your head come to on the door-frame?" Motts tried to gauge where the hooded figure stood by the door. "If we know roughly how tall he is, we might eliminate some of the suspects."

"I'll go check." River dashed to the front door and back in a matter of seconds. "I'd say he's about my height, maybe a hair taller."

"Mikey's shorter than you. Jasper and Ashby are both about your height."

"As are loads of other men and women in Cornwall." He selected one of the remaining buns. "Good news is, Mikey's in the clear. One less person to prod for an answer. Ran into Hughie on my way through the village. He said they'd managed to verify his alibi; he definitely wasn't in the area the week Nadine was reported missing. How in the world did he remember what he was doing three years ago? I'm fuzzy on yesterday, never mind years."

"Prodding probes potentially problematic." Motts decided to grab the last bao before her cousin finished them off. "No idea. I've already forgotten what happened when I woke up."

"It's called getting older."

"Ignoring you." Motts grabbed the receipt from the table to show him. "I found this under the carpet. I'm guessing whoever broke in dropped it while fending off Cactus's attack. Think Nish could figure it out?"

"Cash payment? Standard order with nothing fancy? Maybe. I doubt it." River grabbed his phone and snapped a photo. "Never hurts to ask."

Getting River out of her hair took an hour; Motts finally had time to clean. She'd had the lock to her front door changed and gotten a spare set of keys for her cousin. Always good for someone to have an extra key. She planned to regain her sense of security by thoroughly organising and wiping down everything in the hallway.

She moved each piece of furniture and wall art out into the living room. "Careful, Cactus."

Meow.

"Yes, you're an excellent supervisor." Motts noticed a folded scrap of paper where the coat stand had been. "Where did you come from?"

She didn't remember dropping paper.

Had Cactus's furious attack caused the intruder to drop more than the receipt?

Setting the paper on the kitchen counter, Motts went back to finishing up with her cleaning. She made quick work of dusting everything and then returning all the furniture. After shampooing the carpet, she left it outside to dry on a washing line.

There. Feels as though I've cleared the evil air out of my home. I refuse to be afraid in my cottage.

Motts had just put the duster away when a familiar jaunty whistle caught her attention. She went outside to greet her grandparents. "Hello, you two. I'm fine."

"Never had any doubts." Her granddad pulled a paper sack out of his pocket. "I went by the sweet shop."

"Unlike your granddad, I brought something more filling. Scones." Her gran eased closer to her.

"Is it a hug day? Or are you still bruised from your accident?"

Motts gave her gran a hug and smiled when her granddad held the bag of chocolate buttons out to her. She grabbed a handful. "Are you enjoying the weather? It's lovely and warm."

Her gran ignored her attempt at safe small talk and bustled into the kitchen with Cactus following behind. He meowed loudly at one of his favourite people. "Yes, love. I've brought you a treat as well."

"She's got carrots for Moss and peas for Cactus. And I've got the wire I promised in the boot of the car." Her granddad wrapped his arm around her and held out the bag of chocolate buttons. "How goes your mystery?"

"Granddad."

"Any new clues?"

Sharing the two pieces of paper with her granddad, they inspected the newly found evidence together. A small scrap of paper folded and ripped in half, it appeared to show a partially scribbled telephone number.

But whose?

How do we figure out the complete number?

"What about using the Google?" her granddad suggested. "You can find everything on there."

"The Google?" Motts's mouth started to water when her gran held out a plate with apricot and honey scones slathered with her homemade apricot jam. "Thanks, Gran. Do you use the Google as well?"

After tea and scones with her grandparents, her granddad helped her set up the wire in the garden. She planned to plant peas in the autumn. Her grandparents headed up, leaving her to try and figure out the partial phone number.

Searching on the internet didn't provide any useful information. There weren't enough digits to even make an educated guess. Mott was still perusing websites on how to find phone numbers mid-afternoon when someone knocked on her door.

"Hello." Vina grinned when Motts opened the door. She pushed her way inside. "I brought you a present."

"Have you?" Motts was immediately suspicious when Vina shoved a heavy, large box into her arms. "You shouldn't have?"

"I definitely should have. River and Nish are bringing cold beers and a takeaway along with their movie projector. I've got a sheet we can string up against the cottage." Vina grabbed her by the hand to drag her out into the garden. "Let's set it up."

"Set what up?"

Vina crowded in next to her and ripped off some of the wrapping paper. "Surprise!"

"An inflatable paddling pool?"

"Big enough we can squash in together." Vina nodded enthusiastically.

"A large rectangular inflatable paddling pool." Motts didn't know whether to be happy or mildly annoyed. "Is it even going to fit?"

"I measured."

"Of course you did."

"You need to relax. It's boiling out. You can't solve a mystery when you're melting in the heat and stressed out over a break-in."

MOTTS STARED AT THE EXPANDED POOL. THEY'D moved it into the front of the cottage because she didn't want to risk crushing her plants. "Are you sure four of us will fit?"

"Definitely," Vina promised.

"Not sure Auntie Daisy envisioned this when she left the cottage to me." Motts sat on the edge of the pool with her feet dangling in the cool water. They'd dragged the garden hose around to fill it. "Nish and River are nicking this from you."

"Probably."

"Did you find anything on the receipt?" Motts changed the subject.

"We narrowed it down to a few people who came in while you were there and ordered the same thing. Ashby, of course, which you knew. Jasper. Callie. And another young lad, don't know his name. He works at the O'Connell warehouse." Vina shifted the garden hose out of the way and sat across from Motts. "The bad news is, it doesn't really narrow it down from two of your suspects."

"So, you're useless."

"I brought you a pool." Vina shifted the hose to spray Motts. "At least it proves it wasn't a random stranger trying to steal from you."

No, just a potential murderer breaking into my house. Not comforting.

At all.

"Murdering murderer murders maddeningly." Motts wiped the water from her face.

After Nish and River arrived, they set up the sheet on the outside of the cottage and queued up one of Motts's YouTube playlists. They watched a Try Channel live stream, laughing and eating their weight in takeaway while lounging in the over-crowded pool. They'd almost finished when a police car pulled up.

"Oi. You four degenerates. What's all this racket?" Hughie glowered at them before breaking into a massive grin. "It'll come as no surprise Old Man Orchard called in to complain about the noise even though there's no possible way he can hear you from up here."

"Chips?" River held out a packet to the constable. "While we've got you here, Motts has a number. Can you see if you recognise it? I don't."

"That's not a number. It's a part of one." Hughie tapped his finger against the paper after Motts handed it to him. "Can't say for sure, but I think this belongs to one of the young lads who works part-time for the O'Connells. I rang him the other day about a delivery."

Does it now?

Chapter Twenty-Four

Meow.

Motts peered over her mug of coffee at Cactus, who was lounging on his cushion by the window, having finished his breakfast. "I could try calling the number Hughie gave me last night."

Meow.

"I do hate talking on the phone," Motts agreed. She tapped a finger against the mug. "I could pay another visit to the warehouse. See if this young lad is there."

Meow.

"No, I shouldn't go alone. Though I'm sure I'll be fine if I stay away from the freezers." Motts shivered at the icy memory. "Marnie might be up and about this morning."

Grabbing her phone, Motts sent a text to her. Marnie claimed to be closed for inventory. She told Motts to swing by on her way to the warehouse so she could join her.

After changing into something other than the comfy pyjamas she lived in most days, Motts made her way into the village. She wasn't surprised to find Marnie waiting outside the shop for her with two cups in hand. *Someone's already been to Griffin Brews and probably gossiped about our upcoming adventure.*

Nothing ever stayed secret in a small village, particularly amongst friends.

"Vina says to stay away from freezers." Marnie handed one of the cups to her. "Nish suggested avoiding the O'Connells full stop."

"Not surprised." Motts sipped her favourite chai, made perfectly. She loved the twins. "Did you tell Perry?"

"No." Marnie winked. She waited for Motts to step up beside her before starting to walk. "Being married to a detective inspector has taught me the value of discretion."

Says the biggest gossip in the village.

Ironically ironic irony.

"I don't even have to hear your thoughts to know they're rude." Marnie saluted Motts with her cup.

"Anyway, I overhead Hugh mentioning the number you found. So I imagine Perry already knew, and I don't need to say anything to him."

They meandered through the village. It was early enough tourists hadn't invaded yet. Motts sipped her coffee, watching Marnie enthusiastically greet everyone they met on the way.

"Isn't it exhausting?" Motts asked when they'd rounded the corner and found themselves alone along the lane by the harbour. "All these people saying hello?"

"Not at all." Marnie shook her head emphatically. "I'd be lost if I didn't have a little chat with everyone. Gets me ready for the day."

"Bizarre."

"We can't all be introverts." Marnie tapped her cup against Motts's. "The world would be a quiet place if we were."

What's wrong with that?

"It's closed." Motts stared at the O'Connell's warehouse in confusion.

"Not closed. Looks abandoned. See all the rubbish by the bins?" Marnie gestured toward the side of the building. "How odd."

The windows were shuttered and doors locked with a chain and padlock. No vehicles in the car park. The local fishermen tended to be up bright and early, so the icehouse was as well.

"I'm calling my Perry." Marnie fumbled with her cup and bag before finally finding it. "Can you toss this in the rubbish for me?"

Motts took the cup and her own toward the rubbish bins. "Maybe they've gone fishing? Hughie mentioned the brothers had a boat."

"No one's out fishing this morning. They're waiting for the tide to change." Marnie tested one of the doors. "Locked up tight."

Motts dropped their cups into the recycling bin. She frowned at the dumpster beside it. It definitely ponged a bit; to be expected given the fish, the docks, and the rubbish. Trash tended to smell. *What's that?* "Marnie."

"What?"

When Motts didn't respond, Marnie stepped over to join her. They stared at the overflowing dumpster. Bags of rubbish both filled and lay around it. None of the refuse seemed to be connected to the warehouse itself; clothing and other personal items spilled out of a few of the bags.

"Strange thing to be hanging out of an icehouse dumpster." Motts gestured to a coat sleeve dangling from underneath the lid. "I can understand them throwing it away. It's a hideous combination of mustard yellow and pea soup green, but why here?"

"Amy O'Connell owns a coat like this. I'd bet my shop on it." Marnie was feverishly typing a message on her phone. "She wore it last week, in fact. Strange, given how boiling the weather's been recently. Perry said not to touch anything."

"I imagine he wondered why we were over here." Motts knew the local inspector would have a few words for them. She stepped closer, trying to get a better view of the coat. Her stomach churned instantly upon peering into the dumpster. "Oh. Bugger."

"Motts?"

"Amy's still wearing her coat." Motts held on to her breakfast by the skin of her teeth. She pulled her shirt up to cover her nose. "You might want to call Perry, not text him."

"Motts. Oh, sweet Jesus." Marnie spotted the lone finger visible from the coat sleeve. "Come away from there."

"Well, I suppose this takes her off my suspect list. Or does it?" Motts wondered what had led to her being thrown away with the rubbish. She stared intently at the items visible in open trash bags. Dolls.

"These were in the O'Connell cottage. This makes no sense whatsoever."

Ashby does have a reason to dislike Amy.

Then again, so do her sons and almost everyone in the village.

While Marnie spoke animatedly on the phone with her husband, Motts inspected the side of the building more carefully. No CCTV cameras. *Convenient.* A spot of oil and tyre tracks drew her attention on the far end of the dumpsters, out of view of the village.

Motts bent down to touch the oil by the dumpster. She grimaced at the greasy texture on her fingers. "Still damp."

"What are you doing?" Marnie had pocketed her phone. "Perry said to move away from the building. They'll be here as soon as they can."

"Don't the police do this at crime scenes?" Motts tried to wipe the oil off on a napkin from her pocket. "I wonder if they can trace what vehicle left this."

Was Amy's body dumped here to point toward Jasper or Mikey to frame them?

Or out of convenience? It can't be a coincidence she's here with all of her dolls. Someone was at her cottage.

"Where are you going?" Marnie glanced up from her phone when Motts started up the street.

"I want to see if Amy's vehicle is at her cottage." Motts jogged by her. "Won't be long."

Making her way through the village to the long stairs leading up to the row of cottages on the west side of Polperro, Motts climbed up the steps as quickly as possible. She felt a strange sense of urgency. *Teo will definitely say this is a terrible idea.*

Motts had no intentions of going inside the cottage or even close to it. She only wanted to see if anything had changed on the outside and if any vehicles were parked outside. "I'll keep out of sight. I'll be perfectly fine."

Why am I talking to myself?

On a scale of bad ideas, Motts thought this probably ranked below allowing Vina to teach her how to tango but over having River cut her hair. Neither had been the best decision. The haircut had been particularly disastrous.

She'd worn a hat for most of that summer holiday.

If I were brave, I'd sneak right up to the cottage.

From her vantage point down the lane, Motts couldn't see any vehicles parked at the O'Connell home—neither Amy's nor the delivery van. Neither Jasper nor Mikey was anywhere to be seen.

I could knock on the door or peer in the window under the guise of being concerned for Amy.

Great plan.

Also, a terrible idea.

Motts dithered at the top of the stairs for a full two minutes. *Maybe I should text Teo? He'll come to investigate with me.* She reached into her pocket for her phone, only to freeze when a hand clamped down on her other wrist. "Mikey."

Mikey had definitely seen better days, with his wrinkled and dirty clothes that had a strange smear on one sleeve. He grabbed desperately on to her arm. "Why are you up here again? It's not safe."

"Pardon?" Motts tried to wiggle free from his hold. "Safe from what?"

"You saw the body."

"I did find your grandmother." Motts struggled to keep calm. She knew from experience panic didn't often show on her face. "You already knew about that."

Vina and Motts had once tested her pulse and blood pressure during various situations and levels of stress. Despite drastic changes in both, it never showed on her face. And then she'd gotten tired of being her own guinea pig, and they'd given up on the experiment.

"Not her. My mum."

I found her too.

Am I a body magnet?

"Right." Motts had tucked her hand into her pocket, absently touching her phone. She missed her old mobile with the buttons. It was harder to make an emergency call on a touchscreen without seeing it or using voice activation. "Well, since it's not safe, I should go. We should go."

"Too late." Mikey's gaze seemed drawn to something or someone behind her. He stepped around in front of her. "He's seen us."

"He?" Motts already knew the answer to her question. Jasper. *Were they both involved in killing their grandmother and mother? Hadn't Teo ruled out Mikey? What about Ashby? Was he telling the truth?* "What happened?"

"Not now. Let me talk to him."

"What've I told you about sticking your nose in my business?" Jasper caught up to them quickly. "You were supposed to sod off out of Polperro."

What?

Jasper tried to push his brother out of the way. "And you. Nosy bint. Where's my sodding necklace? It's mine."

"Jas," Mikey pleaded.

Motts glanced between the siblings. Jasper began screaming at his brother. She wondered if they'd notice if she crept down the stairs away from them. *I should've stayed home in my pyjamas with Cactus and Moss.*

Trying to inch closer to the top of the steps, Motts's movement was halted by Jasper. He grabbed her by the back of her shirt, yanking her backwards. The ice pick in his hand caught her full attention.

Random choice of accessory.

Icy insidious insertion isolates injuries.

Maybe focus on the potential double murderer and not another alliteration.

Jasper glanced sharply over his shoulder when a villager from a nearby cottage called out a morning greeting to them. "We should get into the house. And you're going to sodding tell me where my nan's necklace is."

"I'd rather stay outside. Lovely summer weather. It's good for you." Motts tried to shift away from him, but his iron grip on her didn't loosen. "Why don't I buy you both coffee?"

"Walk. Or I'll leave you bleeding here on the walk for everyone to see." Jasper pressed the ice pick against her side. "Quit drawing unnecessary attention. I'll shove this through your heart."

"And the ice pick isn't going to garner attention?" Motts muttered. She leaned away from the sharp point. "Is this how you killed your grandmother?"

Oh yes, it's the perfect time to ask him about this.

"I never killed the old bint." Jasper nudged her again, forcing her to continue down the lane. "Mum did. I only disposed of the body."

I'm sorry.

What?

The creepy cottage of dolls had transformed into a shell of itself, from suffocating with lace and trim to hollow and empty. Jasper had been busy. Motts could understand why the dumpster by the warehouse had been overflowing.

Shelves lay empty where dolls had been. The living room was devoid of anything but the bare bones. No paintings on the walls. Cushions were taken off the furniture. The carpet had been stripped off the floor, leaving scarred wood underneath.

It felt cold and barren, like the mausoleum where her great-grandparents were buried. Motts had no interest in being interred. She tried to keep on the opposite side of the room from Jasper, putting as much space between them as possible.

"Your skills at home improvement are... unique."

Motts shifted over to the window. It, like everything else, seemed freshly scrubbed clean. "The eau de bleach is particularly strong."

Two brothers, an ice pick, and a pineapple have a standoff.

Jasper held the ice pick loosely in one hand. "We can't let her leave. But first, where's my necklace?"

We?

"The police have it. You've grabbed the wrong person." Motts glanced between the two brothers, wondering if she'd been wrong about Mikey. "Did you both kill your mum?"

"No." Mikey flinched as if physically assaulted by her question. "Kill Mum? I couldn't stand the woman, but I'd never hurt her or anyone else."

"Why didn't I drown you when I had the chance?" Jasper spat at his brother. He gestured wildly with his weapon. "Mum hated you for your choices. Always swanning about with your boyfriend."

Shifting to the right slowly, Motts gripped the chair, watching the two brothers shouting at each other. She considered her options. Dying was most certainly not on the list.

"Why can't you ever do what you're supposed to? Just like Mum and Nan. Always making me do all the sodding work while you get a share of the money for sitting on your arse." Jasper lunged at his brother. "We should've started with you."

Swinging the chair around, Motts cracked Jasper across the head. He dropped like a felled tree, collapsing onto the coffee table. Mikey darted forward to snatch the ice pick.

Motts eyed him warily. "I'm calling the police."

"I've already texted Hughie." He went over to place the ice pick high up on a shelf. "Now it's out of reach. Maybe you can relax? I'm not going to kill you."

Motts grabbed her phone to send a text of her own. She wasn't surprised to see multiple missed messages and calls. "I imagine they'll be here sooner rather than later."

"I—"

A sudden crash cut Mikey off. Motts didn't need to look down the hall to know one of her stalwart police friends had kicked the door in. She glanced over at Mikey, who was pinning Jasper to the floor.

"They're going to yell." She leaned heavily against the wall, trying to catch her breath with the rush of adrenaline slowly dripping away. Teo made it to her first. "Definitely the shouty face."

"What were you thinking?"

Chapter Twenty-Five

"What were you thinking?"

Motts stared blankly up at Detective Inspector Ash from her spot on the grassy cliff across from the cottage. She'd been asked the same question by Teo, Hughie, and now Perry. "Tiny holes through the heart aren't any better than large ones."

Perry chuckled, shaking his head. "You're not wrong. Terrified my Marnie half to death. She barely made any sense when she called me. We couldn't get over from Looe fast enough."

"Why were you in Looe?"

"Investigating." He shook his head when she went to probe further. "Perhaps, having captured a second murderer for us, you might restrain your curiosity until we've done our job?"

"I'll do my best." Motts shifted uneasily at the sight of Teo's worried face. He'd been questioning Mikey in the cottage. Jasper had been taken away by ambulance with Hughie as a guard over him. She tried not to think about whether she'd seriously injured him, even if he'd been trying to kill them. "No promises."

"Why don't we get you home? I'm sure Cactus and Moss are worried about you." Teo offered his hand to her, helping her up to her feet. "I wish you'd messaged me."

"You wish I'd waited for you." Motts shoved her hands into her pockets. It had gotten chilly as clouds rolled in off the sea. "Marnie was already calling Perry when I came up here. I never intended to run into Jasper."

"Hello." Hughie met them on the stairs. "Got Jasper all locked up and taken care of. Congrats, by the way, Detective Inspector. We'll miss you."

Motts watched Hughie continue toward the cottage where Perry was speaking with Mikey. "Why did he say congrats?"

Teo sighed. Deeply.

Motts began the descent toward the village. She kept one hand in her pocket and the other on the railing. "He said 'we'll miss you.' Are you going somewhere?"

"Premature congratulations." Teo placed a hand on her elbow to steady her on the steps. "I've been offered a position up in the north. Run of my own cold case department for much of Yorkshire. A promotion, in essence. Nothing's been decided. My parents would have to move with me, and they haven't made up their minds yet. I can't be too far from them."

"You never said." Motts found herself suddenly exhausted. The adrenaline rush that carried her through the confrontation with Jasper had dripped away like a leaky faucet. "Promotions are good. Not easy to get your own unit or whatever. I'd imagine."

"Not, it's not. I planned to talk with you once we'd wrapped up the investigation here." Teo gripped her elbow more tightly when she tripped on the last step. "Careful. Motts?"

"Home." Motts had run out of words.

Shaking her head when he tried to prompt more out of her, Motts trudged toward the road leading around the village and up the opposite side to her cottage. She heard Teo muttering behind her about his perfectly functioning vehicle. Being trapped in a car in the middle of a tense conversation would've been beyond her ability to cope with.

"Motts?"

She closed the door to her cottage on his question and leaned against it. The day had been too much from start to finish. *Finish? It's barely noon.*

Meow.

Motts opened her eyes to smile down at Cactus, who'd come to sit on her foot. "Hello."

Lifting her fuzzy cat into her arms, Motts went into the living room. She curled up on the chair by the window, dragging a blanket around her. Cactus shifted contently in her lap until he could see out into the garden.

What a bizarre day. What will happen to Mikey with his brother arrested and his mum gone? And where's Ashby run off to?

And when is Teo going to run off?

Is a promotion running off?

Mott sank down further into the cushions, pulling the blanket up to her nose. "It's almost anticlimactic."

Meow.

"Okay. Maybe not anticlimactic. Almost being stabbed with an ice pick is a bit climactic. Is climactic a word we use? Climactic. Climactic. Sounds completely made up." Motts grinned halfheartedly at her purring cat. "A meow is much less complex."

Climactically complex climax.

Sounds like a terrible title for one of those naughty novels Vina reads.

The peace and quiet in her cottage lasted not even an hour. River and Nish arrived, using her cousin's key to get inside. Motts knew news of the arrest would've swept through the village like a tidal wave.

"We brought hot chocolate and steamed buns." River lifted a thermos while Nish carried a Tupperware container. "Mum insisted. Dad made the hot chocolate. Not sure it's as good as yours."

Watching with mild bemusement as her cousin and his boyfriend went around her kitchen as if they owned the place, Motts stayed on the couch. They had things under control. She appreciated their not trying to press her for information.

And they had to be curious.

She would've been.

Motts tucked her legs up under the blanket and gratefully accepted a mug of hot chocolate. "Teo's moving."

"Is he?" Nish sat on her left while River collapsed onto the cushion on her right. "Sounds sudden."

Motts shrugged. "Jasper killed his mum."

"His mum? You mean his nan, right?"

"Nope." Motts sipped the hot chocolate. It wasn't perfect; only her dad could claim that title. "Think his mum killed his nan."

"Pardon?" Nish almost dropped the plate he'd been holding. "They certainly had no love lost between them."

"Mmm," Motts muttered into her mug. "Jasper didn't confess everything before I conked him over the head with a chair."

"Pardon?" Nish did drop the plate onto the coffee table.

"He had an ice pick. He lunged." Motts made a jabbing motion with her hand, careful not to disturb her hot chocolate too much. "Stabby, stabby."

"Stabby stabby?" River turned his head away, coughing into his hand several times. "And you're okay?"

"Eh." She shifted underneath the blanket. It had taken a while for the cold to dissipate despite it being the middle of summer. "Not as shaky as I was when I got home. Found my words again. I'm doing better. Okay is another matter."

River and Nish both squashed her into a hug. Cactus lazily pawed at both of them for jostling him from his safe spot curled in her lap. Motts allowed the embrace for a few seconds before shoving them away.

"So, Teo's moving?"

Motts ignored her cousin's probing question and pathetic attempt at changing the subject. "Shouldn't you be working? Both of you?"

"Just making sure your 'delicate nature' hasn't been too disturbed." River sounded as though he was quoting his mum directly. "Also, trying to decide if we need to have a word with the towering detective."

"Towering Teo?" Motts appreciated the alliteration. "No need."

"Mottsy." Nish leaned against her side.

"We've only been dating off and on. My heart isn't in danger of being broken. Not yet. I'll miss him if he goes." Motts had been heartbroken when her relationship with Vina ended, no matter how amicably. They'd loved each other, still did, though it had thankfully turned into a platonic thing. "I'm sad about the potential we might've had."

"Long-distance—"

Motts cut River off with a sharp shake of her head. "If he stays, we'll see what happens. But long-distance would never work for me. Emails and talking on the phone are far too difficult to manage for me as it is."

"Well, on the plus side, a potential break-up has distracted you from a traumatising run-in with a killer." River leaned away from Motts when she went to elbow him in the side. "Or Jasper's murderous rage has provided an escape from Teo's deserting you."

"Dramatic berk." Motts smacked River on the arm. "Eat a bao."

"The most politely phrased 'shut your trap' I've ever heard." He grinned.

"YOU'LL WANT TO PRUNE BACK SOME OF THE SHRUBBERY around the front of the cottage." Her granddad had come over to help her harvest some of her garden, clear out three of the beds, and plant carrots, fennel, spring onions, and a few varieties of lettuce in preparation for a winter crop. They'd already gotten the netting set up for peas. "How are you doing, poppet?"

"Fine." Motts directed water toward a particularly parched patch of herbs. Her granddad cleared his throat loudly. "I'm getting there."

Working in the outside was cathartic. In the month since Jasper's arrest, life had gotten back to as normal as it ever was for Motts. She'd spent much of her time crafting orders and tending her garden.

"Heard young Mikey came by to visit you last week." Her granddad never shied away from asking her potentially hard questions. "Marnie mentioned it the other day."

"When did you run into Marnie? Buying a wedding dress?" Motts finished up watering her parched plants. She set the watering can into the shed and grabbed her gloves. "He wanted to thank me for the peony bouquet. Never even knew it was for him to help him memorialise his gran. She loved peonies, apparently."

"And your young man?"

"Not my young man." Motts missed Teo since he'd moved. Her heart was only dented, however, not broken. "What does it say if I'm only slightly sad? More like a friend went away."

"He didn't touch your soul, love." Her granddad leaned against the side of the shed. "You wait until you find the right one. What about the other detective? The one from London."

"He's a friend, Granddad. Plus, he's busy working on several cases including Jenny's. Said it might be a few months before he has anything to tell me. Everyone isn't lucky to find something like you and gran have." Motts carefully picked the dead leaves off one of her shrubs. "Soulless soulmates solve silly string."

"Yes, they do." He chuckled. "Come on then. We're almost finished here, and we can sneak by the Salty Seaman for a late lunch."

"We had lunch already."

"An extra one then."

"Aren't you supposed to be on a low-sodium diet?" Motts remembered her grandmother giving him quite a lecture on the subject not even a week ago. "Are fried fish and chips on the menu?"

He waved one of his gardening gloves at her. "You wouldn't deny your dear old granddad a last delicious delicacy, would you?"

Rolling her eyes at him, Motts decided what her grandmother found out later wouldn't hurt her directly. Her granddad seemed to enjoy it when the love of his life caught him with his hand in the proverbial cookie jar. Non-autistics were very strange when it came to relationships.

They finished up in the garden, gathering up her tools to clean and safely store in the shed. Motts quickly returned Cactus and Moss to the cottage for their naps. Her granddad washed his hands and met her by the front door.

"Ready?"

Motts ran into his back when he stopped suddenly. "Granddad."

"You've a visitor." He kissed her on the top of the head. "We'll save the Salty Seaman for another rainy day. Your gran will be waiting for me."

She eyed Teo, who stood by his car. He hadn't mentioned a return trip to Cornwall. "How are the dales?"

"Dalish." Teo reached into the back seat of his car and pulled out a box. "I brought you a collection of chocolate from Kacao. You'd love it. A little chocolatier in Richdale."

"You should've told me you were coming." Motts waved him into the house, laughing when Cactus immediately raced over to climb up the detective and sit on his shoulder. "He missed you."

"I did email you."

"I was having an 'I can't respond to emails' week." Motts shrugged. She accepted the precious package of sweets. "Coffee and chocolate?"

"Of course." Teo followed her into the kitchen, taking a seat at the small table. "We finally got the complete story from Jasper."

"Is that why you're in Cornwall?"

"And picking up the last of my parents' belongings. Moving is a pain, particularly across the country." He leaned back in the chair, petting Cactus, who remained on his shoulder. "You'd know all about that."

"Never again." Motts didn't think she'd ever voluntarily move out of her cottage. She finished up the coffee and set a mug in front of him. "What kind of chocolate is this?"

"Thins."

"Thins?" Motts peeled the lid off the box. "Shards of chocolate?"

There was a mixture of flavours of quite thin strips of chocolate. Motts tried the white chocolate raspberry ripple one first. *Well, I'm going to inhale this entire package.*

"There are truffles as well." Teo gestured toward one of the multiple individual packets within the box. "So, Jasper."

"Yes." Motts had heard through the village grapevine that Jasper had asked to speak with the detectives. "Did he confess to anything new?"

"Not really. Confessed to the murder of his mum and helping her to dispose of his grandmother. He did offer a motive of sorts. Greed. They wanted the run of the family business. And he grew tired of sharing with his mum. I imagine his brother would've been next. As I said, none of his story surprised us. Just nice we won't have a long drawn-out process through the courts." Teo shook his head. He reached out to snag one of the hazelnut praline truffles. "A tragedy."

"It's not tragic," Motts disagreed. "Disgusting. Disgusting dastardly devilish deed. He destroyed his family for money. Money. It wouldn't have bought him anything but hollow comfort. Poor Mikey. I don't know how he copes with all of this. I suppose Ashby helps."

Once the dust had settled, Ashby returned to Cornwall. His relationship with Mikey had progressed. Motts had seen the two strolling along the coastal path a number of times; she thought they both deserved to find some happiness together.

"I made Cactus another sweater." Teo handed her a small bag from his pocket. "It'll be cold enough soon. This'll help on his garden adventures."

Motts blinked at the sudden change of subject. "He's missed you."

"Just Cactus?"

"Moss missed you as well." She grabbed an orange chocolate truffle, enjoying her first bite into the outer shell and the creamy citrus centre within. "We've had a lovely summer."

"Motts."

She stared down at the box of chocolates, not wanting to have the conversation, whatever he'd come to say. "You're lovely. I've missed you. Long-distance relationships don't work for me. And I'm thrilled you had a promotion."

"Motts."

"I'm not moving to Yorkshire. I like my cottage." Motts peered up to his nose. He seemed sad. "Can we not make this unnecessarily awkward? Despite my gift for turning everything into an uncomfortable mess?"

"Motts."

"Yes?" She resisted the urge to chatter about nothing to keep from having an actual conversation.

Teo was silent for several long seconds. "You *are* lovely. I missed you greatly. I hope we'll stay friends."

"Oh. The best of friends." Motts reached across the table to grab his hand. She felt oddly weepy. "The best of friends. Still pleased you wandered down the primrose path with me?"

"Definitely."

Watching Teo drive off a few minutes later, Motts suddenly found her cottage too quiet. The weather had turned gloomy and chilly. She grabbed her raincoat and wellies to trudge down to the café for an early supper.

She paused at the top of the stairs, tilting her head to allow the soft raindrops to hit her face. Dreary days didn't bother her so much. Not in Cornwall with the crashing waves in the distance and the seagulls' complaints carrying on the wind. From gentle drizzles to thunderous storms, they added to the magic of the place.

Drizzling dreary days.

"Hello, Mottsy." Vina breezed by when Motts entered the café, arms loaded with mugs and plates. "Come into the kitchen. Amma's working on a new masterpiece with Nish. You can play taste-tester with River."

"Afternoon, dearie." Leena swept her up into a flour-dusted hug. "Come try these new macarons. Pistachio macarons with a masala chai cream. My Nish is trying to turn them into profiteroles as well."

"Now, we hate to gossip." Vina paused to glare at her brother when he coughed loudly. "Rose at the Salty Seaman claims your granddad mentioned a certain detective. And Marnie thought she saw his vehicle driving up the hill to your cottage."

"And driving away again." Motts accepted the glazed profiterole. "Pistachio glaze on top?"

"Hence the green tint." Nish nodded. "Plus the masala chai cream on the inside."

"Isn't he brilliant?" River grinned at his boyfriend.

Motts watched the two interact. They behaved a lot like her grandparents tended to when together. Playful and clearly falling head over heels for each other. Something she hadn't even felt the hint of with Teo. "Jasper confessed to conspiring with his mum and then killing her."

"Not exactly an earth-shattering revelation." River grabbed another one of the slightly lopsided profiteroles. He tossed a second one gently to Motts. "We assumed he'd done that at the least."

"What did you expect? Him to pull off a mask and go 'I would've gotten away with it except for the pesky autistic with the naked cat'?" Vina finished loading the dishwasher. She wandered over to grab Motts by the hand. "Come on. You can help me close up shop."

After locking up, Vina dimmed the lights slightly. She switched off the open sign. Motts leaned against the counter, waiting for the inevitable.

"Are you all right?" Vina dragged her over to begin putting the chairs into place. "With Teo?"

"Fine." Motts shrugged.

"Fine?"

"I don't know." Motts shoved one of the chairs too hard against the table, almost knocking it to the floor. "Not fine. I'm not...."

"Sobbing into a pint of ice cream?"

"No." Motts shifted the next chair more gently. "I wouldn't mind the ice cream. I was sad. I'll miss him, as I said. Just more like the loss of a dear friend."

"On to the next adventure then." Vina draped her arm across Motts's shoulders. "You never know who's right around the corner."

"With my luck, another set of skeletal remains."

IF MOTTS OFFERED JUST THE RIGHT LEVEL OF MYSTERY and escapism, be sure to check out book three, *Pickled Petunia.*

Want more cosies from Dahlia? Check out the complete **Grasmere Cottage Mystery Trilogy** and her London Podcast Mysteries series, starting with *Cosplay Killer.*

Thanks

Thanks for reading *PIERCED PEONY*. I do hope you enjoyed my story. I appreciate your help in spreading the word, including telling a friend. Before you go, it would mean so much to me if you would take a few minutes to write a review and share how you feel about my story so others may find my work. Reviews really do help readers find books. Please leave a review on your favorite book site.

I wrote my first romance series after a crazy dream about shifters and damsels in distress. I prefer irreverent humour and unconventional characters. An autistic and occasional hermit, my life wouldn't be complete without my husband and my massive collection of books and video games.

Join my newsletter:

http://eepurl.com/QonoX

I would love to hear from you directly, too. Please feel free to email me at dahlia@dahliadonovan.com or check out my website dahliadonovan.com for updates.

Join my reader group:

https://www.facebook.com/groups/110875087616294

facebook.com/dahliadonovan

twitter.com/DahliaDonovan

instagram.com/dahliadonovanauthor

bookbub.com/authors/dahlia-donovan

pinterest.com/dahliadonovan

Acknowledgments

Pierced Peony was written in 2020 when life was incredibly difficult for just about everyone. I have an amazing group of friends who help me during dark moments, lifting my spirits to help me find some joy in writing. I'm so grateful for every single one of them.

A massive thank you to my brilliant betas who take my first draft and help me turn it into something legible. To Becky and Olivia who always have faith in me. To all the fantastic people at Tangled Tree. And also to my beloved hubby, who keeps me from losing my mind while I'm stressing over word counts.

And, lastly, thank you, readers, for following me

on my writing journey. I hope you enjoyed *Pierced Peony*. Motts is a character very close to my heart, and I hope you loved her as much as I do.

As Hot Tree Publishing's first imprint branch, Tangled Tree Publishing aims to bring darker, twisted, more tangled reads to its readers. Established in 2015, they have seen rousing success as a rising publishing house in the industry motivated by their enthusiasm and keen eye for talent. Driving them is their passion for the written word of all genres, but with Tangled Tree Publishing, they're embarking on a whole new adventure with words of mystery, suspense, crime, and thrillers.

Join the growing Hot Tree Group family of authors, promoters, editors, and readers. Become a part of not just a company but an actual family by submitting your manuscript to Tangled Tree Publishing. Know that they will put your interests and book first, and that your voice and brand will always be at the forefront of everything they do.

For more details, head to www.tangledtreepublishing.com.

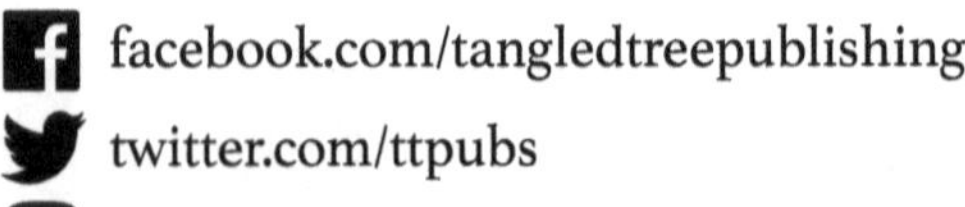